LURKING

LURKING

ALLAN DAVIS

IGUANA

Published by Iguana Books
720 Bathurst Street,
Toronto, ON M5S 2R4

Publisher: Cheryl Hawley
Editors: Lee Parpart and Timothy Rucinski
Front cover design: Ruth Dwight (designplayground.ca)

ISBN 978-1-77180-659-6 (paperback)
ISBN 978-1-77180-658-9 (epub)

This is an original print edition of *Lurking*.

In direct proportion to our degree of willful blindness

In daylight brightness while awake,

The bedbugs come back to bite us

In nighttime darkness while we sleep

Breeding bedbugs out of the dead

Three a.m. is our cruelest hour

ONE

1975

Rebecca

My father threw his suitcase into the back seat of his rusted Chevy Nova. He pulled his coat collar up against the January wind. "I'm sorry, Rebecca." He kneeled for a hug. "Everything's going to work its way out. Wait and see."

I waited to see but I never saw him again. He was replaced by a grey-haired lady who came after school to look after me. For the rest of the winter, my mother managed to hold down a job on the line in the Owen Sound dog food plant. Then one late-March evening, a tall, thin man with longish brown hair and a beard arrived at the door of our one-bedroom basement apartment. My mother introduced him as Leonard Jones, a special friend.

"He's a buyer at the plant." She hung his winter coat in the closet.

"What do you buy?" I asked.

Leonard didn't answer right away. "Horses," he said as he shuffled from one foot to the other, removing his boots. "The plant's not far from the Owen Sound horse auctions. The buyer, which is me, stands next to the auctioneer and bids on each horse."

"What do you do with the horses?"

Again, Leonard didn't answer right away. Then he said, "I can sight the weigh-in within one hundred pounds of any horse led into the ring. Ten cents a pound. If I'm outbid, the horse goes to a new home. If I'm not…"

"Oh." I didn't want to talk to someone who turned horses into dog food.

"That's why I'm going to quit," added Leonard.

"Oh," I said again.

The next Sunday, Leonard arrived with his five-year-old son, Bobby. His ear-flapped hat in one hand, and a red marble game — homemade, it looked like — in the other. My mother's new pills were working better than the last ones, so with my help she had cooked a special roast beef dinner. What is the difference, I wondered — cows turned into roast beef or horses turned into dog food? I ate the potatoes and the green beans but not the roast beef.

Leonard helped my mother with the dishes. I sat in our Goodwill chair next to the Goodwill chesterfield and watched Bobby play his marble game on the floor in the corner. He placed a blue-and-white marble, which looked like an eyeball, in the top part of a trough and watched it run down to the first hole, roll to the next hole, and drop again, clattering and plunking its way from top to bottom. Then he picked up the marble and did the same thing all over again. Although I was wearing my good red dress with white tights, I went over and crouched on the floor beside him.

"I'm eight," I said.

"I'm five," said Bobby.

We took turns with the marble.

"You have long eyelashes," I said. Like a girl, but I didn't say that.

Bobby and Leonard came again for Saturday lunch. They took off their coats and sat on the blue flower-patterned two-seater my mother had got from the Sally Ann. Leonard was dressed in pressed khaki pants and a polo shirt, Bobby in blue pants and a matching sweater. Leonard seemed excited about the farm he'd just bought on

Manitoulin Island, which was where he was from before he started making horses into dog food.

"The farm deal happened by accident." When he folded one long, thin leg over the other, I noticed his socks didn't quite match, both brown but different shades. "I was driving to the island hog plant to apply for a job and I noticed an old house and barn for sale on Pork Chop Road, not too far from the Wikwemikong Reserve. My dog food experience got me the job at the Gore Bay hog plant, so on my way back, I stopped to look at the farm. That was that. I made the down payment and now I'm a farmer."

And then to me, he said, "No more turning horses into dog food."

I wasn't sure why but turning pigs into pork chops seemed better than turning horses into dog food. I liked roast anything, so I decided that turning cows into roast beef was okay too.

Leonard stretched out his long legs and unfolded his long fingers before holding them together in his lap as he settled into the two-seater. "The farmhouse needs work. A coat of paint and new wiring. But the land is good, two hundred acres, half cleared and half bush. I can work at the hog plant until I pay off the mortgage. Then it's fresh air and live-off-the-land: grow vegetables and raise chickens and cut my own firewood and be independent. The simple life."

My mother sat next to him on the edge of the blue easy chair, back straight, face turned towards him. Her pills had made her a little heavy, but wearing her dress with the scooped neck to show the gold necklace she got from her mother, my grandma, dead now, and wearing a little makeup, she looked pretty enough for me to be suspicious.

I said, "Manitoulin Island?"

"Beautiful there." He folded his legs and leaned forward to rest his elbows on his knees. "You go by ferry from Tobermory. The locals are called Haweaters because of the hawberry bushes that grow wild everywhere with little red berries they make into jam, chutney, ketchup, and wine."

"You go by boat?"

"There are two ways: either the Chi-Cheemaun ferry to South Baymouth or the single-lane swing bridge in Little Current. Most people, if they're born there, they stay there."

He nodded, as though agreeing with himself. "The island is in my blood, I guess. That's where I belong."

After lunch, while he talked to my mother about the fresh air and grow-your-own food, Bobby and I sat at the kitchen table, me drawing the pictures, and Bobby, bent over with his crayons, colouring them in. Those long eyelashes. I wanted to give him a hug.

"Look how well they get along," said Leonard. "It's like they've been friends forever, like soulmates. My mother, Bobby's grandmother, believes in that. You meet someone and it's like you've known them forever. They don't even have to talk. It's like they read each other's minds. It's like they walk in the same footprints. Doublewalkers, they're called."

At first, I thought it was Bobby's long eyelashes that got me. But then, when Leonard said that about Doublewalkers, I knew it was something else.

***

We had packed a lunch. Me and Bobby sat in the back seat of Leonard's '65 Ford Fairlane, bought ten years earlier brand new, he said. He showed me a picture, red with a white top and chrome along the side. Now it looked like rusted-out junk, the same as my father's Nova.

We drove from Owen Sound to Tobermory. My mother, who usually didn't say anything, talked with Leonard the whole way. She was happier than I had ever seen her. We took the Chi-Cheemaun to South Baymouth, my mother standing with Leonard at the rail, smiling into the bitter wind off Georgian Bay. We followed Highway 6 to the gravel road cut-off.

"Pork Chop Road," said Leonard.

"What a cute name," said my mother.

"That's not its real name; it's a regional road with a number I can't remember."

Leonard not knowing the number of the road he was going to live on should have been my second clue, the first being the mismatched socks, the third being the lane that led to Leonard's dream of fresh air and live-off-the-land: potholed mud that took us to a muddier potholed yard. Leonard told Bobby not to step in the puddles, but he did anyway so his sneakers were soaked.

The rickety side porch of the paint-blistered white house where we ate our lunch of ham sandwiches and celery sticks was as cold and grey as everything else about this farm. At the end of the lane stood an old barn with boards missing. It was bare black, the same as the fields straight ahead were bare brown, the same as the bush of bare trees off to my left, the same as the side of the house to my right, bare brown — except where the paint had not yet finished peeling off, it was green.

"For the children," said Leonard. "Did you notice how well they played together in the back seat, Ruth? Already like brother and sister." Looking off, he said, "That's the Pattersons', one farm over. He drives a hog truck. Nice neighbours."

At the farm kitchen door, my mother removed her wet shoes. I removed mine. In the daylight coming through one dusty kitchen window, the walls, cupboards, and ceiling were a slippery yellow, I think from smoke and grease. The linoleum floor was so filthy that my mother put her shoes back on. So did I, before following her into what must have been the living room. With no furniture, it was hard to know for sure. The brown curtains pulled together across the front window blocked out the daylight, except for a thin crack of glimmer, which fell on one framed picture propped upside down against the opposite wall. I stepped closer for a better look. It was Jesus, in a dark robe and white halo, his feet in leather sandals, standing in a field of daisies, one hand out, palm up, as if to say, Come with me.

My mother felt along the wall but found no switch. We started up the gloomy stairway leading to the bedrooms. When her foot tripped on a broken step, she steadied herself on my shoulder to adjust her shoe before continuing along the upper hall to the bathroom where she stared at the grey-ringed tub and the rusted taps of the sink hanging from the wall.

Next, she wandered down the hall, turning each rattly glass knob of each bedroom door and peeking in. In the last one on the left, she raised the blinds, but the added light could not change the blistered linoleum or the yellowed wallpaper or the cracked wall mirror hanging crooked to anything besides blistered and yellowed and cracked and crooked, just like every new pill prescription could not change my mother from blistered and yellowed and cracked and crooked.

"Everything will be fixed by fall," said Leonard. "One room at a time. This will be our room, Ruth. It's the biggest, with the biggest window."

And the cracked mirror, I wanted to say.

But, I thought, maybe Leonard's prescription could suddenly do what the doctor's prescriptions could not: open the curtains on that cracked mirror to let in the sun even when there was none.

I turned. I hadn't heard Bobby climbing the stairs but there he was, coming along the hall, staring at me from under those long lashes. It was like I knew he was coming before I turned. Maybe I had heard him climb the stairs, I don't know. He came into the room and took my hand before he took Leonard's and we three stood together, while my mother, off to one side, looked out the window at the endless brown fields and the black leafless trees along a road that had a number Leonard couldn't remember.

"Pretty soon, Ruthie. Pretty soon all this bare brown will turn green."

No one had ever called her Ruthie before. It was like he was stamping out yesterday's weeds that might be sprouting among the seeds now planted in that glimmer of sun in my mother's clouded mind. He led us along the gloomy hallway, Ruthie following him, and me following her, and Bobby following me.

He pointed as we passed. "That'll be Bobby's room and that'll be Becky's."

No one had ever called me Becky before. At first, I didn't know who he meant. But right away, I liked how it sounded: Rebecca to Becky. Ruth to Ruthie. I squeezed Bobby's hand. It was so little in my palm it reminded me of a Mother's Day card I had made in kindergarten, my tiny fingers in black ink on the white paper. My mother stuck it on the fridge and knelt to hug me. I couldn't help doing the same. "Everything's going to work its way out," I said, hugging Bobby.

We went downstairs. For a closer look at everything, my mother said. The last owner had left empty garbage pails in the mud room, but had left all the garbage in the house. Leonard didn't seem to notice until my mother, holding her nose, began to pick up the empty Cheezies bags, unwashed soup cans, banana peels, apple cores, and other stuff, I don't know what it all was. I could see her mind trying not to write down the hopelessness of this farm idea, then trying to stroke it out after it got written. I was afraid she would take Leonard's farm idea home, and she would take it to bed with her, and she would read it back to herself over and over again all night long, and in the morning decide this farm idea might work. And I would end up looking after her when it didn't work, not in our apartment in Owen Sound, but here in this dirty old farmhouse. She did the same for every new prescription. She would read the instructions over and over to convince herself — and me, I think — that these new pills would work. When they didn't, I would be looking after her in whatever basement apartment we were living, same as before.

But this time seemed different. Of course. The garbage could be picked up. The walls painted. What was broken could be fixed. I saw in her eyes that Leonard's farm idea — not the farm but the *idea* of fresh air and garden vegetables — gave her hope, lifted the blinds of her basement-apartment mind and, unlike the pills, let in a little farmer's wife sun. Yes, yes, that was what was happening.

I'd lived all my life with these once-in-a-while ups, but mostly always the downs that drove my father away. He never figured out, even after trying to track them on a calendar from the Red and White Grocery Store, which day would be which. Me neither. But I learned one thing. The difference between my father and me was I couldn't climb into a rusted-out Nova and leave when things turned bad.

Me and Bobby following, Leonard led my mother through the mud room to the back door. He helped her button her soggy winter coat. On the back porch, he said, "Breathe in deep, Ruthie. Hard work and fresh air cures everything. In six months, you'll be throwing away all those pills. And eating proper food and losing a little weight."

I think Leonard knew right away that he'd tripped. Out of his throat a stumble had come. My mother pulled her coat tighter around her shoulders from the chill of that comment.

I said to Bobby, "That's the end of the farm idea."

I think Leonard heard, for right away he said, "See that tree there? That's an apple tree. Apple crisp is Bobby's favourite dessert. Right, Bobby? And that little building over there is a chicken house. Fresh-laid eggs for breakfast. And over there, you can't see it from here, is the Mindemoya River. Fresh-caught brook trout in the spring."

Leonard took Bobby's hand. I watched them walk across the dead wet grass, headed to either the chicken house or the barn. Bobby was thin and delicate, young for his age, it looked like. Leonard was thin and probably, at Bobby's age, delicate. Because I could see his longish brown hair but not his bushy beard, he did not look like a farmer. Or like someone who turned horses into dog food and pigs into pork chops. He looked like one of those poets from my grade three reader series.

I don't know what he looked like to my mother. But what I think, just a guess, he looked like Jesus in that picture, stood right side up, his hand out, saying, Come with me. But she didn't say anything about Jesus to me. What she said was, "At least he doesn't want to raise pigs." She said that as Bobby and his father disappeared into the barn, leaving us standing there in the mud. When I turned to look at her, I saw that Leonard, who did look like the Jesus in that picture, had parted her curtains more than just a little and raised her blinds more than just an inch and opened her coat more than just two buttons. "Better than that basement apartment with only one burner working on the stove. And better than working the line in the dog food plant."

If Jesus could cure the sick and raise the dead, he could fix my mother. That's what I wanted to think. But I was only eight. And I knew it was more than likely, more than probably, that these life-on-the-farm ideas of "better" that she was trying to warm up on a back burner in her mind would soon turn cold and soon be replaced with thoughts of "worse." That after a month or two on the farm, her mind would cook itself into a porridge of bad thoughts that every morning would send her back to bed with her farmer Jesus turned from right side up back to upside down and her mirror turned from cracked to shattered.

I knew that for sure. What I didn't know, would never have guessed in a thousand years, was how it would happen.

TWO

Rebecca

Burly Boys Movers in Owen Sound wanted two hundred dollars. Leonard said that was too much. He rented a U-Haul and paid a homeless man living in the church two dollars an hour to help load our stuff. Me and Bobby rode with Leonard in the U-Haul. My mother followed in Leonard's rusty Fairlane. We stood at the rail of the Chi-Cheemaun and watched the seagulls gliding along beside us, looking for handouts. It was a warm spring day, the sun sparkling on the water. I would have enjoyed the trip if I didn't know where it was going to end.

Mr. Patterson from the next farm came over and helped move in the furniture. At first, I was afraid of him because he was the biggest man I ever saw. He looked like he could carry in the piano all by himself. We didn't have a piano, but that's how big he was. But when he kneeled on the porch step and played a quick game of marbles with Bobby, I knew he was a nice person.

That was April. My mother seemed to be liking the farm idea. She cleaned while Leonard arranged the furniture, partly his, partly ours, and got the electricity and the furnace working. Bobby and I explored the barn and the chicken house and played the marble game and coloured pictures. Bobby never said much but that was okay. Leonard kept saying he was going to Gore Bay to register me in school but he never got around to it. That was okay too.

By the beginning of May, okay changed to not okay. Overnight, it seemed, my mother forgot the fresh air and the apple crisp. She went to her upstairs room and pulled down the blinds and there she stayed for the rest of the month. At night I could hear her getting up, opening the bedroom door, her trembly-from-pills fingers fastening around those rattly glass knobs, trying not to make a sound as the door unsettled itself from the door jamb, her footsteps on the stairs, pausing at the broken step, the downstairs closet door creaking open, the heavy rustling as she put on her coat and scarf, and then the rattle and rasp of the chain lock on the back door.

From my window, I would see her in the laneway, face hidden in grey shadows as she wandered about the yard, sometimes stopping in the middle of one shuffling step to stare into the darkness of Pork Chop Road, the bedtime pill having now dissolved her mind into such a stew-pot mush of bad thoughts she could not remember where she was. Next thing, Leonard would appear and lead her back to her bed.

Sometimes the best she could do during those nighttime trips was go from her bed to the living room chesterfield where I would find her curled up in the morning.

Leonard would say, "Give her time. She's not a farmer's wife yet, but she'll come around. She had two good days last week. Time cures everything, just like fresh air cures everything."

And some days it seemed to. Mother Ruthie would get out of bed before dawn and clean the house and then get into the Fairlane and drive to the Red and White in Little Current. Sometimes she took Bobby because he liked to watch the big hands of the clock tower above the town hall tick away the time while she loaded bags of fruit and vegetables and meats. She especially liked to bring home Jiffy peanut butter and Cheerios. But then, after a day or two, Ruthie would turn back to Ruth and go back to bed for days.

Leonard mostly worked double shifts at the hog plant to pay off the farm quicker, and was too tired to cook when he got home. So, the meat would stink in the refrigerator and the vegetables would wilt in the crisper and the fruit would rot on the kitchen counter, and Leonard would throw it all away except for the Jiffy peanut butter and the Cheerios. They could make it through each day no matter what. Like Leonard. He ate his bowl of Cheerios for breakfast and a Jiffy peanut butter sandwich for lunch. That was all he needed.

When summer came, me and Bobby caught toads and bugs and explored the barn and the river that separated us from the Pattersons' farm. In the fall, me and Bobby rode the yellow bus to Gore Bay to start school. First, we picked up a boy about ten and then a girl about twelve. At the next stop we picked up a blonde girl who seemed about my age holding the hand of a little boy like Bobby but with short eyelashes.

They took the seat in front of us. She turned and said, "I'm Sarah. He's Edward."

She had shadows under her eyes like my mother. "You bought that old Prentice place. I can see your house from the hayloft. My grandpa takes me up there to look out the little window. He's got hawberry bugs that come back at night to bite him."

"Why?"

"The dead people he killed in the war. To get even they first got into his bed and then got into Edward's bed and then into my bed. This is Edward."

I said, "This is my brother, Bobby. I'm starting grade three and he's starting grade one."

"Same as us," she said. "But Edward has a different mom and I have a different dad."

"Same as us," I said.

I made Jiffy peanut butter sandwiches for myself and Bobby for school lunch until we got tired of peanut butter. But then I continued with it because my mother hadn't gone shopping. That's why the kids at school started to call me Jiffy. After a while, Bobby called me

Jiffy too. After a while, I forgot my name was Becky, just like I had forgotten my name was Rebecca, just like my mother forgot her name was Ruthie. I thought about how a name change could be a me change. I thought if I told the kids at school I played marbles with Bobby every day after school they'd start calling me Marbles. Then in my mind I'd start calling my own self Marbles.

THREE

Rebecca

"Your mother promised to go shopping tomorrow." Leonard was sorting through the refrigerator, trying to put together a breakfast that was not Cheerios.

"She promised that yesterday," I said.

Leonard sat at the kitchen table and took my hand. His fingers were long and thin but his hands were calloused. I thought that in his spare time, if he ever had any, he should write poetry about nature, and then give it to me to read. It would be back-to-the-land stuff about now it was spring, time to plant, well almost, then it was summer, time to grow, and then it was fall, time to harvest.

"In the meantime, Jiffy, my mother — you can call her Grandma, she'll like that — is going to come on weekends to cook warm-up dinners, and Uncle Sam, my older brother, is coming to help too. He knows all about farming."

"Is that the brother that was in the Vietnam War? Bobby told me he's afraid of him. His war stories give him bad dreams."

Leonard sighed. His shoulders sagged. Eyes puffy from lack of sleep, he glanced around, as though for the first time he was seeing how it still was: the yellowed walls and peeling paint and cracked linoleum, no different now than the day we had arrived six months ago. He got up and led me into the living room where Bobby was playing the marble game. Leonard sat in the chair he'd bought from the second-hand in Owen Sound. Even though I was too old for being hoisted up on his knee, I didn't mind, probably because my real dad never did anything like that, and I wanted Leonard to be my dad. I liked how he put his arm around my shoulder. It was not a big arm, but it was strong with hard muscles.

"Dr. Brad is trying to find better pills for your mom," he explained.

I nodded. "It's like her brain is writing bad thoughts on her mind and she lays in bed reading them. What is the point in living, why can't I die, my life is terrible…"

"The pills are going to erase those thoughts, like erasing pages in a diary, so they can change to good thoughts."

"That never happens."

"My job is to help her to write down the good thoughts."

"What good thoughts?"

"If you imagine the good, then the good becomes real. That's how life works."

"Oh," I said.

Leonard had a train switch in his brain, tripping his thoughts and re-tracking them from how it was now to how it was going to be soon. Now was fall. But spring is coming, nice weather on its way, before long we'll have her travelling in a new direction. I settled further into Leonard's lap. I wanted to believe him because I wanted to call him Dad.

***

The fresh air did not turn my mother into a farmer's wife and neither did Dr. Brad's pills. She did not get up early to make any farmer's wife breakfast or serve any farmer's wife supper or do any farmer's wife chores. She didn't tidy or clean or do anything. I thought the least she could do was tuck in Bobby at bedtime, even though he wasn't her son. Or do up Bobby's shoelaces that she had taken from a pair of Leonard's boots and now morning to night dragged past her bedroom door.

So, I did up his shoelaces and I turned on the night light and tucked him in and said good night and gave him his big hug.

I'd say, "Lie down now and close your eyes and show me those long eyelashes."

When I bent down to give him a good-night kiss, I could feel them fluttering against my cheek like little butterflies. In the morning, I got him up and got him his Cheerios and made Jiffy peanut butter sandwiches for lunch. After school on Fridays, I tidied the house as best I could before Grandma, who was as short and sturdy as Leonard was tall and thin, came Saturday mornings to clean everything spic and span and wash the kitchen counter with cleanser and water and bleach to get rid of the ants. And after she did that, she would make casseroles, all the time muttering about how the refrigerator blowing fuses was going to set the house on fire, and the clapboard siding would burn the house to the ground in five minutes, and how in the world was Jiffy supposed to warm up a casserole in that leaky oven, and how in the world did he expect Jiffy, only eight years old, to look after little Bobby and why hasn't somebody bought Bobby new shoelaces.

After lunch at one o'clock, Grandma would turn on the radio and listen to the obituaries. She said, "Uncle Sam owns the backhoe so he gets paid to dig graves."

Bobby asked, "Does he bury dead children?"

"I guess he must."

"Did any children die today?"

I said, "No children died today. Only old people, the same as yesterday."

Grandma opened her purse and showed us pictures of her daughter, Jeannie, who left at sixteen and moved to the city and now lived in Regent Park in Toronto. She looked sturdy-built like Grandma but did not have a round face with double chins underneath. Her smile was like Leonard's, a bit curled up on one side.

She showed us a picture of Leonard standing beside his Ford Fairlane when it was brand new. She sighed, staring at the next picture. She held it out and squinted through her glasses. "Ivan's my oldest. It seems he's always at loose ends."

Then she brought out another picture.

"That's Uncle Sam," said Bobby.

Grandma set the photo of Uncle Sam aside. She stared down at the hand that was holding her teacup, sitting in her lap not moving, except for the thumb that had been resting on the teacup began stroking along its glassy surface as though this thumb had decided by itself that it wanted to rub away a spot of dirt left there from not enough soap in the dishwater.

"His real name is Ronald. They started calling him Uncle Sam from those U.S. military recruiting pictures. That's all he ever talked about, joining the U.S. military. Now he's a gravedigger over at Gore Bay Cemetery."

She put Uncle Sam back into her purse but left the others for me to look at while she moved on to talk about her weekly quilting bee at the Most Holy Name of Jesus Catholic Church in Gore Bay. She named each of the dead church ladies no longer quilting. She knew the exact date each had passed on; may they rest in peace.

"To where?" asked Bobby.

"Heaven, Bobby. Which reminds me, I've been talking with Father Kelly. It's high time you two children started going to church. He said he's going to come over to talk to Leonard about it."

FOUR

Rebecca

Uncle Sam drove up the lane and parked his Dodge Ram pickup in front of the barn. He got out. He was wearing a black T-shirt and dark overalls. His work boots, one bigger than the other, clumped across the yard. He had a limp in his left leg and a carton of cigarettes in the crook of his right arm and a baseball hat slanted over one eye. He was no bigger than Leonard, the two of them tall and skinny with the same bodies. But he seemed bigger.

"Is that how he smells?" I whispered.

Grandma tilted her head to sniff. "My Heavens no, that's the hog plant."

I never really noticed the hog plant smell before. And now that I did, I could not describe it, other than to think, now that I've smelled it, I will never not smell it, as though from now on it would be following me around.

"This is Jiffy," Grandma said.

Uncle Sam stared down at me. "Hold these." He handed me the carton. He reached into the pocket of his plaid shirt for a package of Player's.

"She thinks you brought the smell from the graveyard."

He sniffed and pointed in the direction of the plant. "Like Agent Orange in Nam. After a while, it screws up the smell wires in your brain cells so either you don't notice it no more or it makes you hallucinate."

"What's hallucinate?"

"See ghosts. Imagine things."

"Leonard doesn't smell," I said.

Grandma explained. "That's because he showers and leaves his work clothes at the plant."

When Uncle Sam took out a cigarette from the almost-empty package, I noticed he had a gold ring with a blue stone on the second finger of his left hand.

"Uncle Sam knows about farming," Grandma said.

"My own farm over near Tobacco Lake needs work. But I'm glad to stay a few days to help out here. Except the days they're burning entrails. That stink sets my brain cells on fire."

When he sparked his lighter, I waited for the smell hanging in the air to set my brain on fire but just then the wind shifted and the hog smell was replaced by cigarette smoke. He sucked in a lungful, held a moment, then like steam from a boiling kettle, leaked it out his mouth and nose as he said, "Ain't nothin' I don't know about farm work, by Jeezus. How to fell trees, plow fields, grow crops, everything."

***

Eight o'clock next morning Grandma had gone home, and my mother, who had been wandering about in the night, was back in bed. Leonard was working a single and would be home at four-thirty. I made coffee and brought a cup to Uncle Sam, who had slept on the couch, still wearing his dark overalls and a black T-shirt. He sat up, one eye open, the other closed.

"Might as well get used to it, Jiffy." From a shot glass on the little table next to the living room chair, he picked up what looked like a giant blue-and-white marble. "It's a glass eye, from Vietnam." He turned it in his palm so it was looking up at him. Then he turned it so it was looking at me. Then, with his other hand, he opened the eye hole and slipped it in, still looking at me. "I take it out and keep it at my bedside to make sure no hawberry bugs get into my bed while I'm sleeping."

He picked up the cup of coffee and carried it into the kitchen. He sat in one of the four wooden chairs at the table and stared at me with the marble eye, which was sort of blue grey brown the same as the real eye but in the overhead light had glints in it like tiny sparks. He took out a package of cigarettes, not Player's, one from the carton he had brought. "I buy these Cignals at the Wikwemikong Reserve." He slid his thumbnail along the cellophane. He sparked his lighter and lit the end and sucked in the smoke. With one suck he burned his cigarette a third of the way down. With his second suck, he sucked away another third, and with the third, he sucked the cigarette to almost its end. After one last suck close to almost burning his fingers, and even closer to almost sucking all the air from the kitchen, all that smoke began to leak out of his nose, forcing the air out the windows, leaving only smoke for breathing.

He picked up his cup. He drank his coffee, not by holding the cup by the handle, but with his thumb on one side and his fingers, which were yellow from the smoke, on the other. Then he leaned back in his chair to light a new Cignals, the dead one smoldering in the ashtray, smoke settling over his shoulder before squiggling in ribbons to join the coiled clouds hanging from the ceiling. After another drink and another suck, he leaned his head back and rounded his mouth into an O and blew a smoke ring like a giant Cheerio to hang above his head in a yellow-fogged halo, like the one in that picture of the upside-down Jesus.

That marble eye looking straight at me said, "By Jeezus, yer a cutie."

The cigarette and coffee finished, he slanted his baseball hat over the marble eye and headed off to the fields or the bush or the barn, leaving me in the kitchen.

When Bobby came down wanting to play the marble game, I said no. No marbles today.

***

After a supper of warmed-up Grandma casserole, Leonard took Bobby to the chicken house. They were getting it ready for the baby chicks, leaving me in the kitchen with Uncle Sam. He lit up a Cignals. He hoisted the foot with the big boot up on one chair and pointed for me to sit next to him.

"I was a commando in Vietnam. I joined the U.S. military to fight the commies. The Americans called 'em Charlie. I flew a Cobra, a helicopter with a machine gun that could rip a whole village to pieces, killing everybody — men, women, babies, boys, girls, uncles, aunts, fathers, mothers, dogs, cats, goats."

He dragged on his Cignals.

"I got a silver medal for Bravery in Action in my dresser drawer. My name's even on it: Ronald Jones. Someday, I'll take you to my place and show you."

I had never seen a medal and I did not want to see his. But I did wonder how this medal changed his name from Ronald to Sam.

FIVE

Rebecca

Leonard was working doubles, my mother was staying in her bed, so Uncle Sam had brought his housekeeper, a Vietnamese girl named Mylinh, to cook and clean. She looked about twenty and hardly ever spoke. Bobby and I sat at the kitchen table across from each other, and Mylinh was at the stove cooking rice. Uncle Sam was at the end of the table. He leaned back in his chair and said, "I found Mylinh on a Vietnam roadside. We'd burned down her village and lined everyone up in the ditch and machine-gunned 'em all, aunts and uncles and mothers and fathers, dogs, cats, goats. Only Mylinh and her two older brothers, Viet and Willie Billy, got away."

Uncle Sam hesitated. He reached up to wipe his marble eye with the back of his hand. "I smuggled Mylinh over to Canada from Cambodia in a cargo ship. Viet and Willie Billy came later. Mylinh is staying with me to practise her English so she can get her papers, but Willie Billy and Viet live in their convenience store in Toronto."

Uncle Sam lifted his leg and rested his bad foot boot on the kitchen table.

"You wonder how I got this bad foot. Well, I'll tell you. Trying to escape enemy fire, I backflipped over a barbed wire fence but when my buddy tried to, his shoelace caught in them barbs and Charlie shot him before I could cut him loose. I ripped off his dog tag, that's what you did anytime a marine got left hanging off a barbed wire fence by his shoelace. I escaped by crawling through the elephant grass to a ditch and that's just before I stepped on a U.S. mine that didn't explode right. That's why I still got this foot. The army doctor wanted to cut it off but I said no way, I'm keeping this foot for later. I got up off the operating table and left. I wrapped the foot in rice paddy mud and elephant leaves and tied it up with the shoelace off my buddy that was hanging off the barbed wire fence and it healed up just fine except now this one boot needs to be bigger than the other. I've still got that shoelace. I keep it in the same drawer as my medal. That's why I can't stand the sight of Bobby's shoelaces dragging across the floor. It reminds of my buddy, or what was left of him, after I got him off the fence, and that's why, Jiffy, that's why you damn well better teach Bobby to tie up those shoelaces."

Uncle Sam lifted his boot off the table and got up and turned on the kitchen tap. But instead of getting a glass from the cupboard, he sucked in the water direct from the faucet. He glanced from me to Bobby. "In Vietnam kids go barefoot. Do you know why, Bobby?"

Bobby looked up, blinking his eyelashes at me, wanting me to answer.

"In Nam little boys don't have shoes. Here you got shoes and you got shoelaces to keep them tied up and, by bal'-headed Jeezus, in Nam they don't have eyelashes like a little girl. Next time I look, she'll have you in pigtails."

He turned off the tap and lit a cigarette and refastened his baseball hat to slant lower over the marble eye. From the kitchen window, I watched him cross the yard in a sideways-one-leg limp that tilted him to his left, away from that one boot.

***

Mylinh wasn't much bigger than me and her hair was black as shoe polish. She wore jeans and a blue T-shirt. I had never thought about her never smiling until, the day after she arrived, we went to the Red and White for groceries, I noticed her smile when she saw a woman pushing a little dog in a shopping cart. I saw that her teeth were so white they sparkled. That afternoon I listened to her sing-song humming while she cooked a pot of the rice she'd bought at the Red and White. I'd never heard such a soft, soothing voice.

After cooking the rice, Mylinh sat on the floor and tried to teach Bobby how to double tie his shoelaces: fold the left one into one round loop and fold the right one into one round loop and then tie the two round loops.

"Round like Uncle Sam's smoke rings," Bobby said, sucking in his breath and holding his mouth round to blow them out.

I took Bobby upstairs and helped him untie his shoelaces that, because Mylinh had tied them double looped, he could not untie. I helped him put on his PJs. I turned on his night light and hugged him good night.

When I came back down, Uncle Sam was at the kitchen table reading a paperback war book. He had set his cigarettes on one side and the lighter on the other and the coffee cup in the middle. He had put the bad foot boot on the chair but he dropped the boot to the floor and said, "Come sit on my knee, Jiffy. I'll read you this part about the My Lai massacre where I cut my buddy off the fence."

I shook my head.

He put his bad foot boot back on the chair. "I buy my shoes' laces special made at the Gore Bay Saddle Shop, next to Alice's Ladies' Wear Shoppe, and I get the heel special made at the shoe repair. See that silver thing? It stops the heel from wearing down on one side."

He handed me his empty cup. "Bring me a refill, Jiffy."

I brought him a refill.

"Undo the laces for me, Jiffy."

I reached over and undid the laces.

"Tie 'em back up, Jiffy."

I reached over and tied them up.

"From now on you do the same for Bobby."

He finished his coffee and cigarette and marked the page with a paper clip and tucked the book away on the top shelf of the kitchen cupboard. "I don't want nobody else reading my books," he said. "But I can read the good parts to you Jiffy, by Jeezus, yer a cutie. If you had pigtails you'd look like that girl in the song." He sang the tune. "For the girl, for the girl, with the pigtails in her hair."

He sat down and undid the boot I had just tied. He did it up tighter and tied the leather loops double tight. Then he got up and put the cigarettes in his left shirt pocket with the hand that had on the second finger the gold ring with a blue stone. The lighter he put in the right pocket of his overalls. Then he rinsed his coffee cup in the sink and wiped it clean and put it into the cupboard next to his book. He slanted the brim of his hat over his marble eye and set off. From the kitchen window, I watched sparks fly up from his limp along the lane every time that silver thing on the heel of that special boot hit a stone. Across the field to whatever work him and Leonard were planning he went, whatever needed to be done, picking rocks probably, Uncle Sam giving the orders, by bal'-headed Jeezus, about how to do it.

When Leonard came home from work, I told him about the war stories and about everything else Uncle Sam said. Leonard called Bobby down and brought Uncle Sam and Mylinh back from the barn and into the kitchen. Leonard squared himself against Uncle Sam, me and Bobby and Mylinh watching.

"Bobby's only five years old. He lost his mother when he was three. That's when it started, being afraid of the dark and having nightmares. Stop telling him war stories, especially before bedtime. And don't worry about his shoelaces or his eyelashes. And don't call Jiffy a little cutie."

Uncle Sam gave Leonard a-down-the-nose-no-one-tells-me-what-to-do look. "Bal'-headed Jeezus," said Uncle Sam. "In Nam—"

"Shut up about Nam."

"Well, kiss my ass."

That was when life on the farm for Uncle Sam should have ended. I don't know what Leonard could have done, but almost anything would have been better than what he did. Bobby's eyes were big and wide as he watched his father turn his back and walk away.

Uncle Sam slid back his chair. He took out his pack of Cignals. The spark from his lighter glinted in his marble eye when he held the palm of his hand over the flame to light his Cignals.

"Now you know, Bobby, who is the tough guy and who isn't. It's not hard to tell which is which, who is and who isn't. Do you want to be a tough guy when you grow up, Bobby?"

Bobby grabbed around my waist and held on.

"That war's not over, Bobby. In a few years you'll be drafted to Nam. Might as well get ready for what's coming."

Then the blue-grey-brown marble eye fastened on me, and he said, "By Jeezus, yer a cutie. You remind me of that little girl in the pigtails song." He sang the tune.

SIX

Rebecca

The next day was Sunday. Me and Bobby, along with Sarah and her little brother, Edward, who lived two farms over, went with the Pattersons to the Most Holy Name of Jesus Catholic Church in Gore Bay. Sarah told me and Bobby that her grandfather had finally sold his team of Clydesdales called Dora and Dick as a team, not separated. They couldn't be separated. If one got sold to one person, and the other one to some other person, they'd each call and paw and fuss and finally die because they were a team.

The sign next to the path leading to the church steps said, "The Reverend Father John J. Kelly," and under the name written in black letter it said, "You won't know when the truth will come, but be you prepared, for you will be called, and you will be chosen, and you will be taken."

I couldn't believe it. As we were leaving the church, standing just outside the door, a black car with whitewall tires pulled up and first Sarah's little brother got taken, and then, just like that, Sarah got taken.

I asked Mrs. Patterson, "Chosen for what? Taken where?"

Mrs. Patterson explained, sort of: "All sorts of stories have been floating around, what the truth is I don't know. But they should not have taken those two children from their father and mother, even if they weren't married."

"Where did they get taken to?"

"I don't know, Jiffy. Some foster care place."

Monday at school I heard the stories: the grandpa was coming into Sarah's little brother's room at night feeling under his covers, looking for something. Then the grandpa started coming into Sarah's bedroom at night and feeling under Sarah's covers, looking for something. The girl who sat behind Sarah said the grandpa was sent to jail and Sarah got taken to Sudbury, and she didn't know where Edward got taken to.

***

Bobby was fast asleep and Leonard was working nights at the plant and my mother was in her usual coma and Mylinh had gone back to Uncle Sam's farm. My bedroom doorway darkened and Uncle Sam stepped in. He snapped on the overhead light. "Bobby's got hawberry bugs in his bed. Come and have a look."

I followed Uncle Sam down the hallway to Bobby's room.

Half awake, Bobby looked up at me, not understanding as I shifted him over to one side to sit on the edge of his bed. "We're looking for hawberry bugs."

Uncle Sam turned on his flashlight. "In Nam, they got rid of them by burning down the hut and everything in it. But we can't do that. We have to catch them. Let's have a look." He pulled back Bobby's covers. "So little you can't hardly see 'em, Jiffy. Come down here close and have a look."

I could smell the hawberry wine and the cigarettes and he leaned so close to me I could hear his breathing. His marble eye glinting at me said, "We can make it a game, like the tooth fairy."

He felt along the sheet near Bobby's foot. "Here's one, by Jeezus."

He squished it between his thumb and finger.

"Let's have another look. See if he's got any anywhere else. Here's another one."

He squished it between his thumb and finger.

Uncle Sam wiped his hands on his overalls and then fished two nickels from his pocket. "There you go, Bobby. Five cents for every hawberry bug we catch. We don't want them to get into Jiffy's bed."

Just then I heard my mother's door open and heard her bare feet pad along the hall. Uncle Sam snapped off the light. "Don't tell Leonard about the hawberry bugs. He's got enough to worry about."

SEVEN

Rebecca

To get to the Pattersons', me and Bobby could walk to the end of our lane, down Pork Chop Road and up their lane. Or we could go across the field and cross the river where it was shallow by jumping from rock to rock. Partway across the field, not far from the chicken house, stood a wishing well. There was no bucket and no crank or pulley, but if we dropped in a pebble and leaned over and listened, we could hear it plunk into the water. Maybe other stuff was down there too.

"Dropped by other farm kids a long time ago," I said to Mrs. Patterson. We were sitting in the kitchen waiting for the kettle to boil. Usually, we would sit on the porch but it was the middle of October, too cold.

Mrs. Patterson wore her grey hair in a bun and had a round face. Her body went straight down from her shoulders so the only way you could find her waist was to look at where her apron was tied.

"That farmhouse was built in 1912, Jiffy. All those years, all those other kids, a long time ago."

"But not gone," I said. "Nothing in a well can ever be gone. It has no place to go."

"It's an underground spring. That's where you get your water from, through an underground pipe."

"It tastes funny."

"It's the same water as ours and ours is good."

"It tastes like hog plant," I said.

"That's the smell, Jiffy. It sticks in your nose, even when it's not there."

Bobby asked, "When can we go to the Red and White?"

I explained. "Uncle Sam's been giving Bobby five cents for every hawberry bug he catches in Bobby's bed."

"The natives here call them hawberry bugs, which are the spirits of the dead that come back at night to bite you to get even for whatever you did that you shouldn't have. But they're just ordinary bedbugs. If you had any, your grandma would have found them."

"Uncle Sam has already found ten so now Bobby has fifty cents to spend on those big round candies at the Red and White."

Mrs. Patterson hesitated. She got up and took off her apron and hung it over the chair. She sat down. Finally, she said, "We drink from our own well, Jiffy. When we open our eyes and look, we think we see what's out there beyond the well, but all we see is what's in our own well. Uncle Sam saw a lot of horrible things in Vietnam, whatever they were I don't know, but he's brought these horrible memories and feelings home."

"And they're in his well?"

"In his heart. In his soul. Not everyone believes in heart and soul. Not everyone believes in spirits, especially not spirits that are keeping score and come back to bite you. But I do."

I wanted to say, but Bobby has never done anything bad and besides when I look I don't see any bugs and besides he doesn't have any bites. But then I realized what would happen if I told Mrs. Patterson, especially about the pulling back the bedding and then running his hand up and down Bobby's leg. I don't see any bedbugs but what I would see the next Sunday was the social worker driving up to the front of the church in a black car and Bobby and me would be taken like Sarah and that little brother were taken. Even though we'd done nothing bad. Not that I knew of anyway.

To me this was creepy and scary both at the same time. But Bobby didn't seem to mind because every time Uncle Sam played the game Bobby got three or four nickels to put in his Jiffy peanut butter jar to buy more of the big hard candy at the Red and White. I told Bobby that he wouldn't need to play the game so often if we made the candy last longer by both eating the same one. So first I put one in my mouth and took five sucks and then gave it to Bobby for five sucks, and then back again, sitting in our favourite spot next to a loose floorboard in the hayloft of the Pattersons' barn, passing the candy back and forth until it was sucked to nothing and we started on the second. I'm not sure how we were supposed to do it but that's how we did it.

And I always made sure when leaving the church front door that I was holding Bobby's hand, that our hands were always joined like two ends of the same shoelace. I was always careful when going down the church steps to never say, Do up your shoelace, Bobby, because to kneel down to do it up the way Mylinh had taught him, I would have to let go of his hand.

Back home after church I would look at Bobby sitting with his marble game, watching me from under his long eyelashes, and then when he caught me watching, he'd look down at his marbles rattling top to bottom over and over again. He was like one of those dolls with big eyes and long eyelashes that closed when you lay it down and opened and looked up when you sat it up.

The other girls at school had dolls like that, but I had Bobby. The first day at our new school, I held his hand as we walked up the front walk and along the hallway. "This is my little brother, Bobby," I said. On the way to the river to catch tadpoles, I held his hand and, if we met a fisherman, I would say, "This is Bobby, my little brother."

EIGHT

Rebecca

If I had a diary, here is what I would write about the Pattersons: They have no children of their own. I think that is why Mrs. Patterson fusses over me and Bobby. They live in the perfect house. It is white with a black shingle roof and at the end of the lane is a new barn with Mr. Patterson's eighteen-wheeler parked in front. If we lived there, we would look like a picture in a storybook about two happy grandparents with two happy grandchildren.

"Would you like a cup of tea, Jiffy?"

"Would you like a cup of hot chocolate, Bobby?"

We sit at the table. First, Mrs. Patterson wipes off the counter and then she wipes off the table and then she takes off her glasses and then she fills the kettle with water from a well that is good, no dead-hog taste. Then she brushes my auburn hair that reaches almost to my waist. Then she picks up my hand, first the left and then the right, one by one clipping and cleaning my fingernails. I listen to the water begin to boil and then I wait for the kettle to click off and then I watch Mrs. Patterson pour the water.

"Would you like a cup of tea, Earl?"

Bobby and Mr. Patterson get their drinks in Truckers' mugs, but she serves the tea to me and her in Queen Anne teacups over one hundred years old. Just think of all the people who have drunk from these cups, maybe duchesses, princesses or even queens. After tea she washes the cups but not the teapot. She just rinses it out and dries it and puts it away in a corner buffet with drawers filled with frothy-laced dollies and white tablecloths ironed flat.

Saturday afternoons, on the television upstairs, her and I watch movies about old England with ladies in petticoats and parasols, while on the downstairs television, Mr. Patterson and Bobby watch action movies with car chases.

Sometimes Bobby brings his marble game. So, Mr. Patterson, like a giant six-year-old in trucker overalls, like the organ grinder's monkey that wore a little British-style hat and a blue shirt and matching denim overalls with big pockets and there, tucked under his chin, a red bowtie like Sarah's little brother wore to church, that's how comical Mr. Patterson looks sitting on the floor next to Bobby rolling the marbles down the tiny playground slides, zig-zagging end to end with Bobby at the bottom hole catching each one, up and down, top to bottom.

All this I could write in my diary if I had one.

***

Uncle Sam got called by the township to drive the snowplow. Mylinh went to Toronto to help her brothers. Things slowed down at the hog plant and Leonard went back on days. I almost forgot about the bedbugs. My mother was able to manage without Grandma. Sort of.

"What grade are you in now, Jiffy?" My mother was sitting at the table eating lunch. Her eyes were as glassy as Uncle Sam's marble and her face was puffy. When she dropped her Kraft Dinner off her fork onto the floor, she said, "Oops. Where's the dog to keep the floor clean?"

"We don't have a dog."

Her face went blank as Grandma's rolled flat pie dough. "Oh. I thought we had a dog."

But at least she was sitting up and walking around. She even packed our lunches, usually baloney sandwiches with lettuce.

Grandma had made Bobby a birthday cake, I made him a card, and Leonard bought him a set of children's illustrated Danny the Turtle stories about Danny hiding in the grass, peeking out, watching everyone's secrets.

Although me and Bobby usually wandered over to the Pattersons' whenever we felt like it, the next day, me and Bobby got a special invitation. Mr. Patterson gave Bobby a card that said, "For Bobby on his first farm birthday. Six years old." On the outside of the wrapped box the size of a chicken crate, Mr. Patterson wrote, "Long Haul Trucker. Happy Birthday, Bobby."

Bobby sat on the floor to take out the eighteen-wheeler.

"It's the same as Mr. Patterson's hog truck," said Mrs. Patterson. "So you can haul hogs to the plant, the same as him, and park it in front of the barn, same as him."

"I don't have a barn," said Bobby.

"Well, let me see." She opened the door to the basement and brought out another box the size of a chicken crate: a plastic barn and a package of plastic pigs.

***

Mr. Patterson's heart wasn't feeling too good, so Father Kelly came in his black car to take Bobby and me to church, me wearing my blue coat with a red scarf and mittens.

"Look at you, Rebecca," said Father Kelly. "All dressed up and wrapped like Christmas."

The name startled me. I had not been called Rebecca for so long I couldn't figure out who he was talking about. I looked at him closely. He wore all black with a long topcoat pulled tight around his bulging belly. When he bent over and stamped his feet to make sure that he'd brushed off the snow that had fallen during the night, his black fur cap slipped from his bald head and fell to the floor.

Father Kelly said, "You're the closest to the ground, Bobby. Could you pick it up for me?"

Me and Bobby sat in the front pew with the other children — but not Sarah and her little brother who'd been taken to Sudbury and then who knows where. Father Kelly talked about the baby Jesus, who lay snuggly wrapped in swaddling covers in the manger of a barn.

"Those swaddling covers probably had bedbugs," I whispered to Bobby.

I held Bobby's hand leaving the church and didn't stop checking up and down for the black car with whitewall tires until we arrived home. Father Kelly came in to check on my mother who was baking cookies when we arrived.

"Oh look, bal'-headed Jeezus is here," said Bobby, seeing Uncle Sam's pickup drive up the lane.

"Stopped by for a drink but I can't stay," he said. "Got to keep the roads open, by Jeezus."

"If you've been drinking you shouldn't be driving," said Father Kelly.

I waited for Kiss my ass, but it didn't come.

Christmas was the best ever. Me and Bobby and Leonard cut and decorated a tree. My mother, up and around like Leonard's Ruthie, made the Christmas dinner. Out from under the tree came the presents, all stuff we needed that Leonard picked up at the church Christmas bazaar, mitts and socks and stuff, but that was okay.

No more bedbugs.

After Christmas, Leonard went back on double shifts. And then, like Mr. Patterson, Grandma's heart wasn't working right, so she came only every other weekend. Back to bed went my mother. Back to making peanut butter sandwiches for school lunch went me. It seemed to be much stickier than I remembered, hard to slick down on the bread, and harder to wipe off the counter, like the hog plant smell that followed me around, hard to shut out of the house and harder to wipe out of my nose.

Our first winter at the farm melted into spring, Leonard's Ruthie still curled up in her winter coat on her bed day and night, and Uncle

Sam back to get this farm up and running, by Jeezus. "Let's have a look, Bobby, see if you got any hawberry bugs. Here's one, by Jeezus. Keep still while I catch it. Fetch the peanut butter jar. Here's another one. We don't want them getting into Jiffy's bed."

I don't know where Mylinh was, at her brothers', I think. Even if she'd seen Uncle Sam feeling under Bobby's covers and catching Bobby's bedbugs, it wouldn't have mattered. I asked her if she believed bedbugs come back at night to bite little boys because of the bad things they've done, but she didn't know what I was talking about. She said all little boys in Nam had bedbugs and somebody had to catch them. Otherwise, they'd have to burn the house down.

Because I was always there when Uncle Sam caught the bedbugs, Bobby didn't seem to mind. I don't know. Maybe he thought they were like the ladybugs that he'd catch in the field. For sure he liked those nickels adding up in his jar. And the extra tuck-in he got when Uncle Sam was finished.

***

In the spring sunshine on the side porch, me and Mrs. Patterson sipped at our tea, watching Mr. Patterson and Bobby wash the truck. Mr. Patterson, who'd got pills for his heart and a spray nitro thing, and was told to take it easy, still stood big as a grain silo in the lane like Farmer Fireman with a power hose blasting dirt off the trailer after soaping it down with a long-handled brush. Bobby's job was to polish the chrome bumper and chrome wheels.

Mrs. Patterson was president of the local Child Find. There was no place at the back of a hog truck to post pictures of lost children where they wouldn't get dirty, so they got posted on the side of the cab after it was clean.

"You see, Jiffy, first people will notice the hogs squealing and grunting in the trailer. Then they'll notice the shiny chrome wheels and then the shiny cab and then the child's picture. Or first they notice the hog truck and then they look to see the hogs and then feel sorry for the hogs and then they see the picture and then they feel sorry for the child, and then they phone in the donation. So even though it's a hog truck, or maybe *because* it's a hog truck, it's good advertising for disappeared children."

Slaughterhouse hogs and disappeared children on the same truck reminded me of turning horses into dog food, and that reminded me of the first day I meet Leonard and Bobby, and that reminded me of the day my father left in his Chevy Nova and that made me say, "Those children have sick mothers, and dads that run off, and uncles and grandfathers who treat them bad so they run away to find a better place to live. Or their parents are split up and their new parents are stepmother and father, and the stepchildren run off to try and find the parent that left. But the kids are so mixed up they can't because the parents are all mixed up, the person called the father isn't the real father and the person called the mother isn't the real mother."

Mrs. Patterson set down her cup of tea. "Why do you say that about the children, Jiffy?"

"Or maybe the children run off because they've got bedbugs in their beds."

"Why are you still worrying about bedbugs, Jiffy?"

"It wouldn't matter how far the children ran or how long they stayed disappeared, they couldn't get away from the bedbugs."

"What do you mean by that, Jiffy?"

"Uncle Sam says he doesn't want bedbugs getting into my bed."

By this time Mrs. Patterson had forgotten about her tea. She leaned forward, and took my hand. "What do you mean by that, Jiffy?"

"The kids at school say Sarah was sent to Sudbury, and her little brother, they didn't know what happened to him. Sent somewhere else. But no one knows what they did to get sent away in the first place."

Mrs. Patterson leaned back with her tea. "Sarah has been moved to live with her aunt in Toronto. Her brother was harder to place, so he was taken to a group home in Manitoba. They'll be well looked after."

Like the children from Vietnam? I wanted to say. The television showed pictures, brothers and sisters lined up in a row wearing grey clothes and sad faces because no parents stood next to them to look after them. The children weren't missing. Their parents were missing, probably shot by Uncle Sam. Mrs. Patterson stood up in church each Sunday to ask people for money to bring to Canada some of these Vietnamese children made orphans because of the war. Mrs. Patterson also gave pictures of children missing from the Wikwemikong Reserve to Mr. Patterson to hand out at the Truckers' Association meeting so the truckers would paste them on the back of their trailers.

I thought about the pictures of those kids on all those trucks. This made me think of Sarah and her little brother, not pasted on the back of Mr. Patterson's truck but sent to foster care, which seemed to be not much better. I thought that before this had happened, before the social worker had come to take them, somebody should have been paying attention to the warning sign on Father Kelly's church and been prepared for what was coming and should have rescued them before it came. Words on signs are like words on a note to yourself where you write down what to do and then do it. Words written in black on a sign are not so you can look back and see what you should have done but didn't. That's like instead of doing what the words say to do, you leave the words on the sign and do nothing.

If I had a diary, I could draw a picture-sign of Uncle Sam leaning over Bobby's bed, feeling around, catching his bedbugs. And then I could rip out that page and set it on fire and watch the bedbugs drift away in smoke. And then look back in my diary and that picture would be gone, disappeared like one of Uncle Sam's cigarettes into the smoke. Or, by drawing a picture of the sign and then ripping out the page and then in the bathroom flushing the picture down the toilet, then that picture would be gone, disappeared like used toilet paper into the septic. But because that church sign was bolted to two posts stuck in concrete, it was there every Sunday when I arrived for church as a reminder that I had better be ready because Bobby and I were going to be called and we would be chosen and we would be taken.

So, what I did do every morning, like wiping away the peanut butter on the kitchen counter and scrubbing away the grease marks on the stove, I scrubbed and wiped Uncle Sam's smoke and hawberry smell off Bobby's sheets, like using Grandma's Spic and Span to wipe off the kitchen table, and then rinsing out the rag in the sink, like Grandma putting the bed back to Spic and Span. This was better than doing nothing.

NINE

Rebecca

For my ninth birthday, Mr. and Mrs. Patterson took me to Frank's Family Grill in Gore Bay for lunch. It was a warm spring day with not much smell from the plant. The roads were clear of snow and the fields were showing patches of green. After, when they dropped me off in our lane, Mrs. Patterson handed me a present wrapped in white paper with a blue ribbon. Inside, on the first page of the diary, she had written: "May all your entries be good ones."

But, as I climbed out of the car to spend the rest of my birthday with Leonard and Bobby, the wind shifted and the hog plant smell of burning entrails filled the yard.

Dear Diary: I had a bad birthday because Mylinh was still at Viet's convenience store and Uncle Sam was drunk and Leonard got mad because Mother wouldn't get out of bed to bake me a cake. Leonard said something to Uncle Sam who said, "Well kiss my ass" and then he went back to his own farm leaving Leonard to do all the farm work himself.

Dear Diary: Leonard called Dr. Brad who said my mother should be in an institution but Leonard said that would be like locking her up in the 999 Queen Street nut house with grey walls and bars on the windows.

Then the wind shifted and the entrails lifted.

Dear Diary: Grandma's heart is better and as long as she has her nitro spray handy for if she has an attack she can be here permanent. Leonard is on four to twelve so he can do farm work days so it doesn't matter that Uncle Sam is busy grave digging. Lots of people needing to get buried. Everything is better enough that me and Bobby have ham sandwiches with lettuce for lunch.

Dear Diary: Bobby and Leonard do the exact same thing every afternoon. Leonard puts on his jacket and goes onto the porch and down the steps and into the yard. He stands beside his rusty Fairlane and opens the door and before he gets in to drive to work he turns and waves at Bobby watching at the kitchen window.

Dear Diary: Grandma likes her cup of tea at three o'clock every day. I serve it the way Mrs. Patterson taught me. But not in cups drunk from by kings or queens. The cups I use are from the same owner who left all the garbage. But Grandma doesn't mind.

Dear Diary: Grandma sits with her cup of tea and talks about the old days on the island. Her brother (Bobby's great uncle) married a native girl and got into the drink. But he learned his lesson and gave it up when he cut his leg off with his chainsaw. Grandma could see that one coming.

I asked, "See what coming?"

Grandma sipped her cup of tea and then put it down. "It's called reckoning," she said. "Whatever wrong you do, it will come back to bite you. Lots of times you can see it coming, right there in front of you. Sometimes you can't see it at all, but you just know reckoning is on the way."

"Like hawberry bugs in Bobby's bed?"

"The hawberry bugs of the Anishinabek legends? I guess. But I don't see how that applies to Bobby. He's done nothing that needs reckoning."

But then Grandma thought for a minute. She picked up her cup of tea. We went upstairs. She adjusted her glasses and scowled down and adjusted her glasses some more and searched along the bottom sheet of Bobby's bed and then uncovered the mattress. "Not a one. There's no hawberry bugs here." She put the bed back together.

Bobby asked, "If I have them in my bed, will Jiffy get them in her bed?"

Grandma set her cup of tea on the dresser. "If they're in one bed, they're in all the beds. They travel around. But you don't have any. So don't bother your head about it."

"But you said you can see them coming?"

"Well, not really with your eyes. It's not just with eyes that we see."

"But you said you could see the chainsaw accident coming."

Grandma picked up her cup of tea. She sat on the edge of the bed. I saw that her thumb was rubbing at the spot of dirt on her cup the way it had when she showed me pictures of Uncle Sam, in the exact same way she rubbed and scrubbed the kitchen counter clean, in the exact same way I had been rubbing the smoke and hawberry off Bobby's sheets. So then, I realized that she knew that even if the hawberry bugs weren't in my bed yet, she could see them coming but not with her eyes but the same way Uncle Sam was seeing, not with his eye.

Grandma got up. Me and Bobby followed her down the stairs into the kitchen where she opened the cupboard and brought out two candles: "'Doublewalkers. The name Doublewalkers sounds like doubletrees for horses, how they got harnessed together. Remember? Sarah's grandfather had a team of Clydesdales called Dora and Dick. They couldn't be separated. If one got took away, the one left behind would call and paw and fuss until the other got back. You and Bobby are like Dora and Dick. Like twin flames. When twin flames come together they become one. You think one another's thoughts and you know one another's mind and you share one another's secrets and you give energy to one another the same way twin flames give light to one another. That's what's happening here, Jiffy, with you and Bobby. The minute I saw you two together I could see you were Doublewalkers, not with my eyes, but I could see it and knew no matter what, no matter what was coming, you two would never be separated."

Grandma set the candles on the kitchen table. "You set them side by side." She lit the candles. "When you each blow out your candle, you can watch your secret wishes and dreams leave and go up through the ceiling and into the special place where the wishes and dreams and secrets of Doublewalkers get stored away and kept safe to be used later, when needed."

Bobby asked, "Do the wishes float away like Uncle Sam's cigarette smoke?"

"No, Bobby. Cigarette smoke doesn't go anyplace. It sticks to the ceiling and stays there and turns everything yellow. Like smoke that comes back at you. You can't get rid of it no way, except get a bucket of water and scrub it away with cleanser and bleach."

TEN

Rebecca

Eight o'clock each morning, I sat on the top step of the side porch, Bobby in my lap. The breeze from the field was clean, no hog smell blowing his hair to one side as he waited for the slow-blinking, yellow-signal lights of his father's car returning from the twelve to eight. I wrote it in my diary: Bobby sits there, waiting and watching. First the Fairlane will show through the tall trees lining Pork Chop Road. Then it will drop down out of sight into the dip where the road crosses the river. Then almost right away it will come back on this side of the bridge with lights blinking like morris code telling Bobby his father is home.

The mirror on my mother's wall was still cracked and what Leonard thought he could turn into a flower was still a vegetable. When Dr. Brad came with some different pills, he checked out Grandma's heart. "You're working too hard here, Mrs. Jones, and your heart is not strong enough for what you're doing. The nitro spray is to stop an episode when it happens but if you don't push yourself it won't happen."

He saw my half-burned candles on the table that I had been using for Bobby's wishes at tuck-in and he said, "You shouldn't let these children play with candles. This is an old house, too many things here are not safe."

So after that, when I tucked Bobby in at bedtime, I put one hand on the switch of his bedside lamp and one cupped around the light bulb as though it was a candle and told him to make our wish that we'd never be separated. He made the wish and then I made the wish and then I blew out the light bulb and gave him his hug.

After that, for good measure, I wrote it in my diary: I hope my wish goes where it's supposed to and doesn't get twisted like Uncle Sam's cigarette smoke when the rings break against the ceiling and turn backwards on me and comes back to bite me.

But back to bite me my wish came. Leonard would not give up his dream of seeds to be planted and crops to be harvested. He did his farm work from eight in the morning to dark, slept a few hours and then left for his twelve to eight. But there was always more needed to be done. Grandma could only come every other day. Mylinh was working at her brother's convenience store. Then Leonard got put back on doubles and Uncle Sam got laid off at the cemetery. I was sitting on the porch step when he pulled up the lane. So I wouldn't have to talk to him, I got up and headed for the barn. Because the sun was behind me, I walked on the heels of my shadow, my legs stepping when it stepped, my foot falling when it fell, as if I was following the footsteps of some other me leading me along the lane away from the house. I thought, if I am the one following, who is the one leading? If this is what's coming, why am I following?

I turned the other way and crossed the field to the Pattersons'. I found Bobby playing with his truck in the corner. Mr. Patterson was sitting at the end of the table, his big hands and thick fingers gripping his little pencil, adding up his receipts and expenses for his hog truck. Sometimes, Mr. Patterson rubbed his hands together because his fingers got sore from writing with a too-small pencil.

Mrs. Patterson sat me at one end of the kitchen table and began to brush my hair. She would brush until it sparkled in the sunshine.

I said to Mr. Patterson, "You should use one of those big fat ones, like Bobby's."

He looked over at Bobby. He said to Mrs. Patterson, "Tell Bobby what happened in the Red and White."

Mrs. Patterson smiled. "I'm involved with Animal Rescue as well as Child Find, which is how I met a border collie called Nellie. She was a seeing-eye dog for a blind man who was big and clumsy. He should have been more careful. One day he stepped on Nellie's paw and broke her ankle. But he didn't know it until a lady saw Nellie in the Red and White hobbling along with a broken leg, still guiding the blind man. So she phoned Animal Rescue who phoned me."

Mr. Patterson opened the door to the basement and into the kitchen limped a black and white dog. Nellie looked at each of us in turn and then went straight to Bobby who hugged her so hard she almost choked.

***

I wrote in my diary: Mr. Patterson has a kind face and brown eyes that get soft like sadness when he watches Bobby playing with Nellie. But they harden like anger when Bobby talks about Uncle Sam telling us war stories. I want to tell about the bedbugs before Bobby lets it out. I know he will. Like Grandma could see the chainsaw coming, I could see that shadow leading me and I could see those big fingers of Mr. Patterson following me and I could see those big hands picking up Uncle Sam by the neck and those big arms slamming him down on the table and his big voice saying, What's this I hear about you looking for bedbugs in Jiffy's bed?

Sure enough, Bobby said, "Uncle Sam says he's the Bedbug Fairy."

Mrs. Patterson examined his arms and neck and my arms and neck. "If you had bedbugs, you'd have bites."

"Maybe they bite other places."

"You don't have bedbugs," said Mrs. Patterson.

"Except the one upstairs," said Mr. Patterson.

"Don't say that in front of the children. God bless her, it's not her fault, it's all those pills they feed her, mixing her brain up so she can't tell imagine from real."

"Bedbugs in the brain," muttered Mr. Patterson.

Mrs. Patterson looked at me and said, "Jiffy, you're holding your stomach. Are you not feeling well?"

I had not realized I was holding my stomach. I had not realized I had a sore stomach. It seemed to have just arrived, maybe when I saw Uncle Sam turn in the lane, or now that I was thinking about it, more than probably when I saw that shadow walking in front of me.

The concern I saw in Mrs. Patterson's eyes, so different from my mother's blank stare, almost made me blurt out the truth.

But I said, "I guess I get stomach aches from the smell."

"Usually, we don't get the east wind, but even a light breeze will do it."

"I can smell it at my house but not here."

"As Earl says, it's the smell of printing paycheques."

Mr. Patterson got up. "She shouldn't be getting stomach aches. I think I'll go over, Emma, and have a look."

"No you won't, Earl. You stay away from Sam."

"Same answer. I'm going over."

"No you aren't, Earl. Don't stress your heart. I'll go over."

The springtime breeze that drifted across the Pattersons' fields was different from the hog smell wind that blew across Leonard's fields. That same spring they found that boy buried under Pork Chop Road a twister had ripped a weeping willow over onto a second tree and the roots ripped from the ground and knotted into a fist of knuckles and fingers like the one in the pit of my stomach. Under the willow's roots was a hole about six feet deep and four feet across. I imagined on the day that Mr. Patterson found out that the bedbugs in Uncle Sam's brain were going to crawl into my bed, Mr. Patterson would come over and drag Uncle Sam across the field and dump him headfirst into that hole and that fist of roots would wrap around Uncle Sam's bad foot so when Mr. Patterson stood the tree up straight it would bury Uncle Sam upside down in that fist of tree roots.

But luckily it was Mrs. Patterson who came over and luckily Uncle Sam wasn't there. She put on her glasses and searched Bobby's bed and my bed with her flashlight. "Not a one. He's imagining things." Then she said, "Let's see how your mother is doing."

It's like I'd forgot about her. Bobby and I were away all day at school and after at the Pattersons'. We'd watched a movie where a boy kept his dead mother in the attic. Sometimes he'd go up and talk to her. But I never talked to my mother, so if she died in her room, I wouldn't know it.

"My Lord." Mrs. Patterson stared down at the heap of blankets. She raised the blinds and opened the window to let out a smell worse than the hog plant. She poked and pulled at the pile of blankets until my mother's head appeared. Then the rest of her, oh my God, naked as the white slugs Bobby found under rocks and poked at to watch them squirm. It was like a pile of rags on the floor got a poke and what appeared was a naked person.

"Who's been looking after her, Jiffy?"

"Leonard gave up but he won't let them put her away. Grandma gets her up and feeds her. She has bad days and better days. On bad days she wants to be left alone."

When the paramedics came they took her vital signs and sat her up and dressed her and took her away. Mrs. Patterson took her bedding back to her house to wash in steaming water with bleach.

***

I was at one end of the table drawing pictures for Bobby to colour, and Uncle Sam and Leonard were at the other drinking coffee. They were talking about the new union contract. The hog plant workers were going after more money and holidays and everyone to get five hundred thousand dollars life insurance.

"Now you're worth more dead than alive," said Uncle Sam, reading the union paper. His marble eye narrowed and glinted the way it did when he looked for bedbugs.

He lit a cigarette. When he sucked in the smoke, I listened to it circulate through all those little green pea lung sacks that got boiled into grey mush when the U.S. airplane by accident dropped chemicals on his platoon. Their brains too, I guess.

Then I noticed that, at the exact moment Leonard mentioned a payout of a million dollars for accidental death, Uncle Sam's grey mush brain began to find a way to get that money. I could see by looking through the glass of that marble eye that his brain was in there working out a plan. It was like I was watching Uncle Sam sitting in his own head, staring into his own cigarette smoke, looking at a picture of himself framed in one of his own round smoke rings, the million dollars in the same hand that had the gold ring on one finger.

The next day, when Leonard came home, he sat us all down at the table for an announcement. "The contract got passed."

I counted the rings. Usually, there were only three or four, but as Leonard explained to Uncle Sam that the hog plant workers got what they wanted, including the big insurance policy, Uncle Sam blew out seven smoke rings. Then he and Leonard walked across the fields and into the trees where the new second-hand tractor and wagon and chain waited, ready to pull out stumps, Uncle Sam giving the orders, deciding how it would be done, by Jeezus.

Next day, Bobby was on a hog run with Mr. Patterson, and Leonard and Uncle Sam were in the chicken house catching deer mice and I came into the kitchen from outside and found Grandma collapsed on the floor, a rag in one hand, a carton of Old Dutch in the other, and the nitro spray still in her purse. I pried open her mouth and sprayed in two spurts but she wouldn't wake up. I phoned Dr. Brad who phoned the ambulance to take her to the Espanola hospital.

Mrs. Patterson came over and sat on the chesterfield next to me. "Take a minute or two now and tell me your best memories of Grandma and then tuck them away in your mind, somewhere safe so they won't slip away on you."

I wrote in my diary: Grandma is here in my mind like all the stuff we did together happened yesterday and all the stuff she told me about candles and wishes and Doublewalkers. All of it real and none of it not real. I don't want to wipe any of it away. Not about Grandma.

ELEVEN

Rebecca

For a while, everything was pretty good, maybe because now, with Grandma gone, at every tuck-in, Bobby and I could light the candles and make the wishes. Leonard worked only days, no weekends. Mylinh was with us to help until my mother came back.

Mylinh and me and Bobby were sitting in the grass watching Uncle Sam and Leonard pick rocks from the field, which the frost brought up that spring. Bobby explained to Mylinh, "If there are any of Mrs. Patterson's missing children buried there, the frost will bring them up and lay them there in the field with the rocks. I'll tell Mrs. Patterson and she'll come over to see which one it is so she can take the picture off Mr. Patterson's hog truck and give me the reward."

Mylinh started to cry, I guess because this reminded her of her dead brothers and sisters and cousins. Or, who knows what it reminded her of. But I saw that she had her own hawberry bugs that came at night to bite her because, when the breeze shifted and she lifted her head to test the wind like Nellie sometimes did, I saw fright come into her eyes as she searched all around, looking for I don't know what, whatever she could see, I guess. But Bobby caught on. He took her hand and pointed up Pork Chop Road. I don't think she understood until, when he sat down in the grass, not worried about it, and began to poke at a toad, she figured out it wasn't the U.S. army dropping Agent Orange, it was the plant shifting from hocks to entrails, which smelled like rotting bodies.

And then up Pork Chop Road came the rust-red Fairlane with my mother. "This is our new Ruth." Leonard put his arm around her. He smiled and gave her a hug. He'd bought her a nice bottle of Chanel to go with a new outfit to come home in. Her hair was clean, not plastered down the way I remembered. Her face wasn't puffy. She looked pretty good. Well, sprayed-with-air-freshener good, meaning better than how she was.

***

When I found a loose stone in the wall of the wishing well, I pulled it out and looked inside, and there was a little hidey-hole. That's where I hid the diary so Uncle Sam wouldn't find it. That's where I wrote everything in it in secret, sitting in the long grass and leaning my back against the stone wall. It was like having a conversation with myself that no one else could hear. I didn't want to talk to myself about bedbugs or hawberry bugs. Not even about ladybugs. But sometimes I dreamed that Uncle Sam came sneaking into my room, although he never actually did. What did come sneaking in at night was the smell of entrails, and if my eyes had been open, I might have seen that shadow I had followed along the lane standing at the foot of my bed.

The day the police came to take Sarah and her little brother, Mrs. Patterson had said, "They weren't real brother and sister and the parents weren't legal man and wife. That was a big problem. If they had been properly married with their names written down on proper papers, they wouldn't have been split up and sent to different places."

So I wrote in my diary that if I ever met someone I liked well enough to live with, I would make sure I got married so everyone's names would be the same and I'd make sure my kids didn't have one name and then another name and then get nicknamed after something you buy at the Red and White. I would make sure the papers were signed so Child Find could find the children if they went missing without needing to paste them on the back of eighteen-wheelers, and I'd make sure there were no uncles or grandfathers living with us, and I'd make sure I would never do anything wrong enough for any dead cousin to come at night and stand at the foot of my bed. Well, I don't think I had any cousins. Maybe Bobby had cousins somewhere but Leonard had never mentioned that. Maybe that shadow was a Bobby cousin no one knew about.

I wanted my diary entries to be good: my mother a happy farmer's wife out of bed cooking a farmer's breakfast, Leonard a happy farmer working the fields, Bobby a happy farm kid playing with Nellie, a happy farm dog. I thought if I wrote the good days on the right page, and then, if there was a bad day, like Uncle Sam coming on a weekend with no one else home, I could write that in pencil on the left, so I could erase it after he left. Like spraying with air freshener after the bathroom.

But, like Grandma said, Bobby and I were Doublewalkers. My thoughts were his thoughts. He could read my thoughts and feel my worries. So I knew he could not keep quiet about the bedbugs. I could see it coming.

"When are we going to the Red and White?"

"Why do you want to go to the Red and White?" asked Mr. Patterson.

"To buy the big hard candy with the money I got from the Bedbug Fairy."

"And who is that?" asked Mr. Patterson.

I said, "Leonard bought a wood stove because the wiring in our house is old, from probably in 1912, he said, when the house was built. So we can't run electric heaters."

"What's that got to do with the Bedbug Fairy?"

Bobby said, "If the wood stove burned the house down that would kill the bedbugs."

"That would do it," said Mr. Patterson. And then he said, "I think I'll come over for another look. See if I can find any bedbugs."

Mrs. Patterson said, "I think not, Earl. One of the conditions on Ruth being home was that Mylinh be there looking after the children. She'll get the feeling we're checking up on her. From now on, we mind our own business and stay out of it." And then she said, "I saw Ruth and her in the Red and White doing the groceries. Mylinh has a lovely smile. And looks after little Bobby like he was her own."

The bedbugs, the hog smell, the shadow, the stomach aches, and now the Pattersons are staying out of it. I could write it all in pencil and erase it but this would not change how it was going to be. That wouldn't change anything if it was coming.

Some days, sitting by the well, I didn't need to write anything and spent my time flipping back to the bad entries, which is why, since Ruth was back walking around and Mylinh was there and everything was fine, I decided I should drop the diary into the water and the bedbugs and the smell and the shadow would drown and they would never come back as long as I never again came back to this well. Then I would forget about them, and the stomach aches would go away.

Then I thought I should learn to be like Mylinh. She's had way more than smells and bedbugs and stomach aches to deal with. She must have lots of shadows to deal with. But she was thankful just to have a place to sleep, even if it was the pull-out in the living room.

TWELVE

Bobby

I left a marble on the kitchen floor and Uncle Sam stepped on it and twisted his foot. So he grabbed all the marbles and one by one pitched them into the tall grass.

My dad saw him do it. "Pick up Bobby's marbles."

My dad's arms and shoulders were brown from working in an undershirt under the hot June sun. He held the pointed end of a crowbar in his right hand. The bent end was hanging like an upside-down cane.

Uncle Sam one by one picked up the marbles. He handed them one at a time to my dad — one, two, three. My dad passed them one at a time to me — one, two, three — all but the blue-grey-brown one. It still lay somewhere in the grass.

"Where's the blue-grey-brown one?" I said.

My dad said, "Bobby wants the blue-grey-brown one."

"Well, Bobby can kiss my ass."

They stood like two roosters waiting for who would make the first move. Daddy didn't answer. He looked away like Mrs. Patterson did when I asked a question she couldn't find an answer for until she put the kettle on. My dad said, "You can find that one yourself, Bobby." And he walked across the field, back to the tree stumps.

Standing, my eyes were level with Uncle Sam's belt buckle. If I looked up past the belt buckle, I saw his stubbly chin and bushy eyebrows but not the marble eye. When he was looking for bedbugs with his flashlight shining down on me all I could see was the marble eye, almost the same as the blue-grey-brown marble lost in the grass. So now when Uncle Sam was catching bedbugs, I thought he'd found my marble and was using it for an eye instead of his own marble eye. But I wanted that marble for my marble game.

The only way to kill the bedbugs was to burn the house down and then live at the Pattersons. To make a fire big enough to kill those bedbugs I would need to gather lots of papers and empty cigarette packages and sticks and dead branches and dry leaves and cardboard, gather it all up. So I did. And hid it behind the chicken house. But the rain next day got everything wet. And when I sneaked the *Manitoulin News* from the living room in the night, the wind blew it away. The next day I found dead wood and dry sticks in the spruce trees by the river. The branches were thick so I could hardly get to the dry parts. When I did, my legs and arms were covered with pricks and scratches. But by the river, I found a wooden Coca-Cola box, so I put my fire-making stuff in the Coca-Cola box and hid it behind the barn. That afternoon near the fence by the wishing well, I found a piece of plywood for a lid. To stop it from blowing off, I put a stone on top. Now I had lots of dry paper and sticks and pieces of wood no matter how windy or wet it got.

The next day was dry. I opened the box and took out newspaper, sticks and pieces of cardboard. In the back field out of sight behind the barn, I ripped and crumpled the paper. I put on the cardboard and sticks and leaves and pieces of wood. On top, I put Uncle Sam's war books. I thought about dragging Uncle Sam's chair from the kitchen, clunk clunk down the porch steps and across the yard. But his was the biggest chair. If Jiffy or I sat in it, he'd tell us to move. Jiffy said my dad had given him that chair and he should never have done that.

When I lit the match, fire jumped in forks, shapes danced in yellow flames. I sat in front, up close, to watch bits of burned Charlies float off like black feathers riding the smoke. Pretty soon the last book had burned away, and the fire was almost gone, and the afternoon had turned grey, and there was no warmth left. I lay in the grass and felt through the wool of my heavy sweater Uncle Sam's cold fingers creeping from the dirt.

"Bobby, what are you doing?"

I sat up.

Jiffy stamped out the fire that had spread into the grass. "You'll burn the barn down. And what is this?" The toe of her shoe poked at a half-burned book. "You burned his war books? Oh my God, Bobby."

Jiffy sat beside me. "We'll say we don't know what happened to them. He'll look in the cupboard and say, 'what happened to my war books,' and you say you don't know." She took my hand. "I know. Say my mother took them. With her new pills she's not remembering anything. She won't remember if she did but if we say she did she'll think she did."

THIRTEEN

Rebecca

Ruth was doing fine. The new pills were working. Mylinh was needed at Viet's convenience store. Dr. Brad said okay. Mylinh and I hugged each other, like sisters almost. Hugs with Bobby made her cry.

But the day after she left, while Leonard was doing a double, Ruth wasn't feeling well. Uncle Sam said, "Go back to bed. I'll take them with me to Gore Bay to get a haircut." On the way he said, "We can stop at Stella's to get yer hair changed into pigtails."

"Pigtails? I have to ask Mrs. Patterson."

"I asked yer mother. She said, put it in pigtails. Grandma used to say that hairstyle is too old for Jiffy. It's not suitable for church. That's how yer mother got the idea. She said to me, take Jiffy to Stella's in Gore Bay and get her to put in pigtails that are suitable for church."

"Mrs. Patterson likes it the way it is."

"Tell Mrs. Patterson to kiss my ass."

It was a hot June day. Uncle Sam drove with the window of his Dodge Ram down, his arm out the window, his baseball hat slanted against the sun. After Bobby and Uncle Sam got their hair cut at the barber, we went to Stella's.

"Nothing fancy, Stella. Like ordinary pigtails like in the song. You know the one I mean?"

"Of course. The Pigtail Polka." Stella hummed the tune.

Next, he drove to the Wikwemikong Reserve to buy a box of cigarettes from Tug Wilson, who lived in a little house in a weed-filled yard with a pickup with no wheels and a tractor with two flat tires in the front yard. Each box had ten cartons of Cignals; each carton had ten packages. On the front of each package was a man's face with a feather sticking straight up between two braids hanging below his shoulders.

Then he drove to his farmhouse, which was like Leonard's but fixed up nicer. Me and Bobby sat side by side on the living room chesterfield and watched a rented VCR movie about a girl about seven wearing knee socks and a short skirt. Her hair was in pigtails and she sang the pigtail song with three other little girls in pigtails.

Uncle Sam took the cigarettes out of the box and him and Bobby laid them face up, like poker cards on the kitchen table. "Two hundred Cignals all in a row," said Uncle Sam. He liked lining things up in rows.

"I buy a pack for fifty cents, sell it to Viet for seventy-five. He sells it in his store for a dollar, which is cheaper than buying regular cigarettes for a dollar fifty."

He sat down with a bottle of hawberry wine. "Have a drink with me, Jiffy."

"We have to go. My mother will be wondering."

He drank some hawberry. His marble eye looked straight at me and said, "By Jeezus, yer a cutie in yer new pigtails."

My stomach gave a turn and my nose filled up with the hog smell. "Bobby has to go to the bathroom."

I took Bobby's hand and led him to the upstairs bathroom and shut the door. "Go down and tell him I'm sick and I'm going to puke and I have to go home."

The next thing I heard from downstairs was the door banging shut. I looked out the window and they were in the truck, waiting for me.

***

Early next morning, my mother still in bed, Uncle Sam, who'd stayed over, was in the bathroom shaving. I stood at my bedroom window and watched Leonard climb into the Fairlane to drive to Little Current to buy a chain and a crowbar for pulling stumps. From my bedroom window, I watched Bobby standing in the patch of early morning sun, waving goodbye to his father.

Uncle Sam's square-trimmed haircut had left a white line across the back of his neck. When he noticed me staring at another white line, this one through his cheek whiskers, he said, "You looking at this scar? A piece of shrapnel went through my cheek right here, feel it, and knocked out one tooth here, feel it, and came out up here, took out my eye here, feel it."

I shook my head.

In the kitchen, he took a bottle of hawberry from the cupboard and set it on the table. As he twisted the corkscrew into the neck, he broke off a chunk. He twisted in again to dig it out.

"Homemade," he said. "Sometimes the cork don't come out right."

He offered me some but I said no.

"I'll put it in a glass," he said.

It looked like the same glass he put his marble eye in when he didn't put it in a shot glass.

"I learned how to make rice wine in Vietnam."

He took a long drink and swished it around in his mouth. I waited for the wine to come up and out his glass eye. But his throat went up in a swallow and down the gullet into the stomach went the wine.

"But this ain't rice wine, this is hawberry wine. They make it on the Wikwemikong Reserve. Six pints of water and a little lemon juice, add the raisins. Raisins are good for you. Try it, it's good."

He poured more into the glass.

"In Nam, girls yer age, nine, ten, are already grown up, cooking the meals, looking after their little brothers and sisters. Here you don't need to grow up so fast."

"I look after Bobby."

"Where is Bobby?"

"I think he went over to the Pattersons'."

He leaned back in his chair, waiting for me to drink. He adjusted his baseball hat, which now with the new haircut was riding on his ears. I sniffed the drink, which smelled like the vinegar water Grandma used for washing windows before she died.

"It's good for stomach aches. Any time I get one, I take a glass or two of hawberry. It's an old Manitoulin recipe that they used to sell at the drugstore. You know in Gore Bay on the corner where the Chinese restaurant is, that used to be a drugstore. They'd have hawberry in the window with a sign, 'good for stomach aches.'"

I picked up the glass and brought it to my lips for a taste.

"That's not enough. You got to take a good belt."

I drank a little more and held it in my mouth.

"That's it. That's good. Now swallow."

I swallowed, gagged, put the glass back on the table.

He drank three more gulps. I listened to the gurgle in his mouth. I listened to the glunk glunk of the wine going down his throat. He topped up my glass, a rusty red on the grey Arborite tabletop.

"You got to drink it. You don't know how it feels until you drink it." He crossed the big boot with the silver heel over his knee and sat back in his chair and waited, his marble eye in the sunlight glinting at me from under his tilted baseball visor.

"On the bottle, it used to say, two glassfuls to take away yer tummy blues." He sang it to the tune of the pigtails song. "Two glassfuls take away the tummy blues."

This time I took too much and choked, coughing closed-mouthed at first and then doubled over. After I caught my breath, I wiped my eyes and face with a dish towel.

"Pretty good stuff, eh? Homebrew." He took his package of cigarettes from his shirt pocket and lit one. The smoke coiled in a haze above his head before drifting across the kitchen ceiling.

"Come sit on my knee."

I shook my head.

"In Vietnam, they got big families all living in one room. Girls yer age look after their brothers and sisters and do the cooking and cleaning. Here you can stay young as long as you want."

"I look after Bobby."

"The wine looks good on you. It puts a blush on yer cheeks."

A blush in my cheeks? Yes! That's what it felt like. Because the wine had made me glow inside. More important, it had taken away the knotted ache behind my belly button. It seemed that ache had been there so tight for so long I thought my skin was going to split and my insides spill out on the floor. I thought, two glassfuls takes away the tummy blues. I hummed the tune to myself: two glassfuls takes away the tummy blues.

When we heard Leonard's Fairlane come up the lane, Uncle Sam put away the wine bottle and rinsed the glasses. I made Leonard his lunch of baloney sandwiches and celery sticks, and Leonard left for the four to twelve.

From the bottom of the stairs, Uncle Sam called up to my mother. "I got work to do at home. Jiffy's gonna help."

I was sure my mother would say no. Still groggy from the wine, I was trying to put together an excuse when he called up again, "What do you think, Ruth? Bobby could use a little time with his new-found mother."

She came down. "I was planning to bake a birthday cake with Jiffy."

"She already had her birthday."

"She did? When? Jiffy, why didn't you tell me?"

I didn't answer. I was more than groggy. I was seeing a double mother standing before me and a double Uncle Sam holding the door for me and a double Uncle Sam climbing into his Dodge Ram.

He climbed in. "The chicken house is ready, by Jeezus, the cash corn has begun to sprout, cord on cord of firewood cut and ready for sale, fields cleared of stone. Cleared the land with these hands, by Jeezus."

Uncle Sam held them for me to see. "I get these fingers into the soil, Jiffy, I feel the soil with each finger, smell 'em, Jiffy." He held his hands out for me to smell. "Like Leonard says, the smell of a free man. You bury the seed and down comes the rain and up comes the crops and in comes the money."

Well, by Jeezus, driving the whole way with the windows down, no hog smell in the wind. I didn't have a baseball hat tilted or a cigarette hanging between sips of hawberry, but I felt like I did.

"Yer getting to like the wine, grows on you, looks good on you. How's them stomach aches?"

They were definitely gone.

"Yer a pretty little girl," he said. "Prettier than those girls at school, I bet."

When he said this, I got a jolt in the grogginess.

"When we get to my place you can help me check under all my bed covers to make sure there's no hawberry bugs."

By the time he'd parked his pickup and led the way to the back door, the hawberry wine fog was gone, replaced by the smell of entrails. It filled the house, not just at the doorway or in the kitchen but oozing out of everywhere, hanging from the ceiling in the bathroom even, where I'd gone immediately and closed and locked the door.

I sat, closed and locked in the bathroom darkness on the toilet trying to figure out what next. Going to the little window and opening the curtain, I saw the grey boards and stone foundation of Uncle Sam's barn, and in the reflection from the windowpane, I saw the blue bedspread and pillow of my bed at home. I remembered that first Sarah's grandfather pretended to be looking for something in her little brother's bed and then he pretended to look for something in her bed. I remembered that Sunday standing at the church door when the black car drove up, the same shade of black as the letter on that sign and then Sarah and her little brother got taken, just like the sign said.

Mrs. Patterson said Sarah had been taken from Sudbury to live with an aunt in Toronto, which was better than foster care. But the little brother was hard to place, said Mrs. Patterson. He went to a group home somewhere in Manitoba.

I said, "I'm feeling sick. I have to go home."

"If you're sick, have another glass of hawberry."

"I'm sick from the hawberry. I'm going to puke."

***

Leonard was standing by the kitchen table, one hand on the back of a chair. "The plant shut down early," he said. Then he asked, "Am I forgetting something? I don't remember giving permission for Jiffy to go to your place." Leonard squinted at me. "What happened to your hair…?"

"Uncle Sam took me to Stella's."

Leonard turned back to Uncle Sam. "Who said you could take Jiffy?"

"Father Kelly told me her hairstyle wasn't suitable for church. He said at her age it should be pigtails." Uncle Sam sparked his lighter and lit his cigarette.

Leonard's face was flushed and his hand on the chair back made a tight fist. I was sure this time it would come. I waited for that chair to fly up and smack into the side of Uncle Sam's head, sending the marble eye flying across the kitchen. I pictured Uncle Sam sitting forever eyeless in his own chair at his own table and drinking his hawberry all by his own self and smoking up his own kitchen with his Cignals all by his own self. He'd have to undo his own boot with the leather shoelaces, put his foot on his own chair, and look for bedbugs in his own bed by his own self and tell his war stories to his own self.

I waited for the swing of Leonard's arm that would make all that happen right before my eyes, me watching, me waiting.

But instead, Leonard slid the chair away, under the table. "I'll have a word with Father Kelly. There was nothing wrong with her hair. In the meantime, let's get this farm up and running."

I went out to the wishing well and I wrote in my diary: Dear Bobby. One day big and little will switch places. You will be big, bigger than Uncle Sam. You will find this diary and read it and you will do to Uncle Sam what your dad could not.

Sitting there, my back against the stone, I closed my eyes and imagined I was hiding under Bobby's eyelashes. I felt myself disappearing into those eyelashes and reappearing in the Pattersons' kitchen telling Mr. Patterson about Uncle Sam wanting to look for bedbugs in my bed. I already knew how he was going to do it with me because I'd watched him doing it with Bobby: running the fingers of his right hand along the inside of my leg and the fingers of his left hand feeling along my back, catching them one by one and squishing them one by one between the thumb and the finger of his hand.

I had my own bedroom and Bobby had his and, although both windows were on the same side of the house, we had two different views. I needed Bobby to know that I could see from my window that if I told anyone about the bedbugs in his bed the police would take just him but I could somehow get him back. But now if I told anyone about bedbugs in my bed, they would take us both and separate us and send me who knows where and him to Manitoba.

How could I explain that the bedbugs in his bed were not about him but about me? He would not understand the alphabet soup of worry and fear in my stomach that I was trying to turn into words and sentences on the pages in my diary. He would not understand. It was bedbugs. But there were no bedbugs. It was the smell. But most days there was no smell. It was a marble eye that could see. On no day can marble eyes see. For Bobby, it was a trip to the Red and White to buy candy.

FOURTEEN

Bobby

Uncle Sam's Dodge Ram pulled up the lane where I played with my truck. The door swung open and Uncle Sam stepped out. He had a Campbell's soup box of new books. He stood them in a row on the hood of the truck where I could see them. They were the same books as the other books that he'd read already. He carried them inside, limping in his one bigger boot, thick leather laces laced up tight swinging past me, not even bothering to look at me with either eye. Up the steps and across the porch and without knocking, he walked right in, as though as well as that chair, and my marble, my dad had given him the whole house.

When Mr. Patterson came to visit, he clumped his work boots up the steps and knocked his fist on the door. When Mrs. Patterson came, she tiptoed up the steps in black shoes that looked like slippers and tap tapped on the glass. Father Kelly climbed one step at a time, his black trousers pushing up against the weight of the Bible held tight to his chest, riding on the shelf of his belly. Usually, he waited at the door, wiping his shiny shoes back and forth on the mat as though he thought the door should be answered without him needing to knock.

Jiffy's mother had bought a mat, so we didn't track mud into the house. Now the mat was covered in mud but everybody still wiped their feet on it. If there was no mud on their shoes before, there was after.

I picked up my truck and the handful of shingles I used for its garage, and I crossed the yard to the kitchen window, which was propped open with a stick. Hanging on to the sill, I pulled myself up to peek through. Jiffy was wearing the white blouse with blue flowers on the front that Mrs. Patterson had bought for her at the Woolworths.

Uncle Sam poured a cup of coffee. He sat in his chair at the table. He asked Jiffy to bring him the sugar. When she handed it to him, he reached out with one finger and traced the lines of the blue flowers. Then, setting down the cup, he tried to pull her onto his knee. Then, from upstairs, I heard Ruth call for help. Jiffy pulled away and, straightening her blouse, disappeared.

Uncle Sam drank his coffee, took out a cigarette, tapped it three times on the front of the package, reached into his shirt pocket for his lighter, flipped the top and sparked the wick. No tiny flame appeared. He flipped the lid down and then flipped up the lid and sparked the lighter again. The flame jumped from the wick and stood straight up, yellow on the outside and blue in the middle. It flickered to one side and then stood straight for him to light his cigarette.

I waited for the red button of the cigarette to get sucked down to his fingers. But he did not blow any smoke rings. He turned his head to listen to the squawk of the chickens that he'd brought home from Tug Wilson's in crates. Uncle Sam had put the hens in the big pen, the two roosters in separate pens. He'd stood at the wire mesh fence and watched them look around, trying to figure out where they were.

Uncle Sam crushed the cigarette into the ashtray, finished his coffee, fastened on his baseball hat, and went onto the porch. He limped down the steps and into the yard, pulling the brim of his hat down against the hot sun because it bothered my marble eye the same as it had his own marble eye. They were both the same, made out of the same kind of glass, and both got hot in the sun. But they didn't melt like those little pigs that came with my hog truck that Mr. Patterson said not to leave in the hot sun.

I followed the lane past the barn and into the field where my father was digging out a tree stump with his crowbar. I came back and played with my truck in the gravely dirt of the lane. I set up two blocks of wood as weigh scales like at the hog plant. I drove over the scale and stopped and then drove off, picking up and delivering the plastic hogs. I poked around in the twitch grass, looking for sticks to start my next fire. I kicked my feet through the long grass along the lane, looking for cigarette packages or bits of cardboard. As I crawled on my hands and knees, looking through the grass with my fingers, I noticed near the front corner of the barn my dad hooking the tractor to a chain wrapped around a stump. Uncle Sam stood next to him, giving the orders of how to do it, by Jeezus. My dad climbed on the tractor and it leaned into the chain and Uncle Sam bent over to pry with the crowbar.

Nellie came down the path. She limped towards me. Her crooked foot seemed more crooked because she was carrying pups. Nellie poked through the grass until she found a toad, and then I cupped the toad in my hands to carry it to the lane to set it down. I wiped toad pee off my fingers with the sleeve of my shirt. I waited until Nellie found another one. I set them side by side in the gravel. Then Nellie poked at one until it hopped, and then the other until it hopped, and after each toad hopped, Nellie hopped and I hopped, and pretty soon everyone was hopping down the lane.

But not all the way to the barn. Nellie was too fat. She lay down in the grass and licked along her belly, which was almost ready for the pups coming in two weeks. After Nellie finished her rest, I hitched her between the handles of the wheelbarrow and climbed in to drive her to the Red and White in Gore Bay to buy candy. But Nellie lay down again. Maybe she'll play fetch, I thought, noticing a stick by the lane. Then I noticed something red in the grass. It looked like Ruth's scarf, the one she threw out the window during her last spell. But when I picked it up, it was a rag, so old and dry that it crumpled to pieces like the scrunched-up paper Jiffy sometimes caught me with. She always took it away, then fished in my pockets to see if I had any matches. She would ask. "What are you planning to do with matches, Bobby?"

"Set fire to the hawberry bugs."

She would look at me. Then she would say, "Wash the toad pee off your hands and do up your shoelaces and don't play with matches."

I would do up my shoelaces and wash my hands and carry my truck to my bedroom and park it under my bed and do whatever else Jiffy said, except the matches part.

Nellie was looking at something, and when I looked, I saw Uncle Sam swing the crowbar sideways, like a baseball bat. It hit my father on the back of the head. He fell backward off the tractor to the ground next to the stump. Uncle Sam was standing by the tractor, the crowbar laying across his shoulder, looking down at my father lying sideways by the tractor wheel.

Uncle Sam knelt beside him. Then right away he limped across the field towards the house. Seeing me in the grass, he stopped. He looked down. I looked up. When he reached for his cigarettes in his shirt pocket, I saw that his underarms were wet with sweat and when he lit the cigarette I saw that his forehead was wet with sweat that must have been leaking into my marble eye because I saw that it had red lines in it now from his wiping it with the back of his hand. I saw that his hat was not slanted sideways like usual but tilted back so that I could see a fly hiding in the shadows of the underside of the brim.

Uncle Sam hurried on, clumping into the house, back in a minute with Jiffy, explaining to her as they walked past what had happened: that Leonard had fell backward off the tractor and hit his head on the wagon hitch.

Uncle Sam hoisted my dad over his shoulder as if he was carrying a wounded vet out of the rice paddies. He rolled him onto the wagon and hooked up the tractor. I watched them drive across the yard to the house, Jiffy sitting by my dad, so he didn't roll off.

Uncle Sam carried him inside.

"Where's Daddy?" I wanted to know when I reached the house.

"He's upstairs in bed," Jiffy explained. "He fell off the tractor and hit his head. But Uncle Sam says he's going to be all right. He was a medic in the marines so he knows how to bandage people up."

"Can I see him?"

"Not now, Bobby. You go outside and play until supper's ready."

My truck coasted across the porch from front to back. It banged to a stop when the bumper hit the wall. I used blocks of wood for houses I set up in two rows to make a town to drive through.

I saw Uncle Sam swing that bar. At least, I thought I did. Maybe it just looked like that. Ruth saw things that didn't happen. She thought things happened that didn't. Maybe that was it. I picked up the truck and let it roll down again, almost running over that same fly sitting near the railing, washing its hands, I was sure that was the same fly that was under the rim of Uncle Sam's hat, so now it was washing its hands that were dirty from what it just saw, stopping for a minute to look around, then washing them some more, like Grandma washed her hands that were dirty from what she just did, like maybe gut a chicken, and then looking to see if there was any chicken blood left that she didn't see the first time and then washing them again.

I left my truck on the porch and walked across the field. The crowbar lay in the grass where Uncle Sam dropped it. The fly was there ahead of me, circling before landing on the blood on the bent end, not hardened yet, stuck on like fresh peanut butter. The fly sat there, licking and wiping, trying to clean it off the crowbar.

Jiffy came from the house. She knelt beside me. She waved away the fly. She said, "What really happened?"

"Uncle Sam knocked him off the tractor with the crowbar."

"Are you sure?"

I nodded.

"Then don't touch it, Bobby. Don't touch the blood." Jiffy got down on hands and knees for a closer look. "What did you see exactly?"

"Uncle Sam swung the crowbar like a baseball bat."

"What was Daddy doing?"

"Sitting on the tractor."

"Then what?"

I picked up a stick and pretended to hit her on the back of the head.

Without touching the crowbar, Jiffy parted the grass for a better look. "You saw, Bobby. You're a witness." She stared at the crowbar.

Sometimes Jiffy's eyes were sad, sometimes worried. Now they looked afraid.

"If someone finds it, they'll phone the police. They'll split us up and send us to foster care. They'll lock my mother up in 999 Queen Street. Or that place in Penetang. But most important, Mr. Patterson will kill Uncle Sam and go to jail forever."

Jiffy picked up the end of the crowbar with no blood on it. "I'm going to hide it where no one will find it. If Uncle Sam asks, say you didn't see anything. And don't tell Mr. Patterson. I've got to figure this out. Don't you say anything. You were playing Toad with Nellie and you didn't see anything."

Jiffy sat in the grass, looking down, one pigtail curled over her shoulder. I leaned over to look up at her. She said, "Uncle Sam says your dad will be all right but he's a liar." She stared at the crowbar. "I think I should phone the ambulance."

I sat in the grass, waiting.

She said, "But then the police will come and put us in foster care."

She put her arm around me and hugged me. Then she picked up the crowbar and set off across the field. After a while, the sun dropped behind the barn, and I felt cold. Jiffy called me for supper.

"Uncle Sam says your dad is sleeping," she whispered. "He says he'll be better in the morning. So don't you worry about it. You know nothing about the crowbar. You don't know where it is, and you don't know anything about it. Give me your hand."

She held it in both hers and squeezed. "What did you see?"

"Nothing."

"Good. Yes, you saw nothing."

FIFTEEN

Bobby

Father Kelly's black car shone in the September sun by our laneway ditch. I cut through the weeds to pick up my truck, its red hood peeking from its garage of broken shingles. The night before I had left it there, where Father Kelly's car was now parked, beside the patch of goldenrod. I waded in and slid down the bank. Pushing through the weeds, the truck in one hand, the shingles in the other, I tripped on my shoelaces. When I reached out to catch myself, my truck scraped the side of Father Kelly's car. I licked my finger and tried to wipe away the long thin scratch. I scrubbed at it with my T-shirt like Grandma scrubbed the kitchen counter.

I saw that the front wheel of the truck's cab had been bent and wouldn't turn. I looked for something to fix it. After banging the wheel with a stick, it still wouldn't work. Finally, I gave up. I carried it along the lane, up the path, across the porch and inside.

The mud room was so dark I had to feel my way to the door, dragging one hand along the firewood piled against one wall, almost covering the window. "Wood for winter," Uncle Sam said. "Take out the furnace. Why buy oil from them crazy Arabs when you got a hunnerd acres of firewood on yer own farm. Tell them Arabs to kiss my ass."

In the kitchen, the sun lay in a square across the linoleum to the refrigerator. I dropped the shingles on the table and carried my truck up the stairs. Ruth was curled up under her covers.

"Father Kelly is here." Jiffy was tugging at her mother's arm, trying to get her up. "He wants to talk to you."

My father's bedroom door was shut. I turned the glass doorknob and walked in. The blinds were partly down, like half-shut eyelids. My father lay on his back in the bed, his blankets pulled up under his chin, his face yellow-grey, like Grandma's candles, his eyes staring at the ceiling.

"Daddy." I pulled at the blankets. "Can you fix this?" I held the cab of the truck above his face. When I tried to turn the wheel, dirt fell onto his cheeks. When I spun the other three wheels, more dirt rolled down along his nose and into his beard. Some rolled into his eyebrows, which were bushy and curled down into his eyelashes. But most fell into his open eyes.

"The wheel won't turn. Watch how it goes." I ran the truck across the blankets, over his chest, and down one leg. "See," I said, coming back and pulling at his arm. "It won't turn."

"Bobby! Come out of there!" Jiffy grabbed my hand and led me out of the room. "Daddy's gone to sleep."

She shut the door. At the bottom of the stairs, she sat on the floor and hugged and rocked me. In the living room, Father Kelly, leaning forward in his chair, talked with Ruth, now buried under a blanket on the couch.

"Sit up, Ruth, so we can figure this out. I can't talk to you, and you can't answer if you're hiding."

Ruth crawled out and sat up, rubbing her eyes into open.

"What are you going to do? How are you going to support yourself and two children? Well, Ruth, you've got the farm. At least you've got a place to live."

"I don't know how to farm." She pulled the blanket around her shoulders. "I hate this stupid farm. I didn't want to come here in the first place. Him and his stupid farm. Now look what happened."

"I don't mean to farm. I mean you have a roof over your head."

"But how am I going to earn money? What are we going to live on?"

"Leonard had life insurance, didn't he?"

"But that's just it." She seemed awake now. "That's the problem. After the strike ended, Sam told Leonard to leave his life insurance to him, as guardian of the children in case anything happened. But the will says everything goes to Bobby when he turns eighteen, nothing in there about any insurance."

She searched around under her blanket until she found a jumble of crumpled papers.

Father Kelly sat on the edge of the couch. "The will is dated four years ago, before he knew you, Ruth. Did he not have these changed?"

Ruth pulled at her blankets. "You know Leonard."

"The insurance by law should go to you. Where is your marriage certificate?"

"I don't know, Father."

Father Kelly glanced through the letters and the papers. "It says here you are Ruth McDermot but the children are Rebecca Johnson and Robert Jones."

"We never got married, Father."

"They are stepchildren, in other words?"

"Rebecca is mine but she kept her father's name. Bobby is from Leonard's first wife. They both go by the name Jones at school. Leonard just never bothered to get it sorted out, you know how he was, Father."

Father Kelly read from the papers. "When I die my estate goes to Bobby. There is nothing here about any guardian."

Father Kelly stopped reading. "Bobby needs a guardian. There's Jeannie. Leonard's sister. We haven't seen her for years. Leonard hasn't seen her for years. Leonard's brother, Ivan, is around, I see him from time to time. And then there's Sam."

Father Kelly sorted through the papers. "The mortgage has life insurance so it will be paid off. A place to live, at least."

"He did this on purpose, forcing me to get a job. I have chronic depression and I'm bipolar. Some days I can't get out of bed. But he didn't understand that. 'Psychiatrists are all quacks,' he said. 'Move to the farm. Fresh air and hard work cures everything,' he said."

She slid herself down into one corner of the couch and closed her eyes.

"This is a problem," Father Kelly nodded. "But I do have some experience with wills. This is one of those do-it-yourself ones, which means it can be contested. Ordinarily, everything goes automatically to the spouse. But…" He slid the pages into the envelope. "You aren't a real spouse. This is a big problem. We'll have to take this to a lawyer and see what can be done about both the will and the insurance. In the meantime, you'll have to get a job in town."

"A job? What kind of job can I get?"

"Any job. What did you do before you came here?"

"I worked on the line at the dog food plant."

"Then get a job in the hog plant."

She pulled her blankets up to her chin.

"No. No. Not back under the blanket." Father Kelly leaned over and pulled off the blanket. "Sit up now. Freshen yourself up a little for when the ambulance comes."

***

The ambulance backed through the weeds to the back porch and stopped on the bare patch in front of the first step. After the two men in blue uniforms carried my dad out on the stretcher, the sheet pulled over his face, Ruth climbed into the front seat. Then the ambulance drove out the lane and down the road, red light flashing through the spinning dust. Finally, beyond the dead elm by the river bank where the crow always sat, the ambulance disappeared.

Father Kelly came into the living room. "What medication is Ruth on, Rebecca? Show me the bottle."

Jiffy sorted through the medicines in the cupboard and handed it to Father Kelly. He examined the label. "Lithium. What are all those other medicines?"

"Grandma's high blood pressure and nitro spray."

"I'm going to ask Dr. Brad about this. In the meantime, I'll phone Emma Patterson to come over and stay with you. Uncle Sam has gone to Toronto to get Mylinh. She knows how to cook and clean and look after children. I assume Aunt Jeannie hasn't been notified so I will try and find her. Anyway, we'll have this all sorted out in no time."

"Where's Daddy gone?"

With a grunt Father Kelly hoisted me into his arms, careful the truck did not dirty his suit jacket. We collapsed onto the nearest chair. "Your daddy's on his way up to Heaven, Bobby."

"Why is he going to Heaven?" I settled myself into the black folds of Father Kelly's lap.

"We don't know why, Bobby. We never want death to come knocking on our door, and we don't know why it comes when it does, but we have to go just the same."

When I leaned my head against his belly, I heard gurgling noises like when the bathtub drain backed up the stink of sewer water.

"How does death come knocking?" Was it like Mrs. Patterson's soft tap tap or Mr. Patterson's heavy knock, knock?

"It comes only once in a lifetime and asks no questions at the door and leaves no footprints on the floor."

"Does death come knocking with a crowbar?"

"No, Bobby. That is not how death comes knocking."

"What does death look like?"

"We don't see death. Our eyes are closed and it comes while we sleep."

"What if our eyes are open?"

"They are shut like in sleep."

"What if they're not shut?"

Father Kelly shifted my weight. "And when they open again, they're in Heaven."

"Where is Heaven?"

Father Kelly took the truck from my hand and put it on the floor. "Let me show you." He pulled out his Bible, hidden somewhere in his priest's suit. He opened to a picture of two men and one woman in long white dresses.

"Why are the men wearing dresses?"

They were standing beside a wide blue river with four boys about Jiffy's age. In a green field grazed seven white sheep. On the other side of the sheep, children dressed in long white dresses sat having a picnic in the grass.

"Why are the men wearing dresses?"

Jiffy said, "Everyone dresses different up there, Bobby."

"They don't have shoes."

"No shoelaces to do up."

"See here these little birds?" Father Kelly said. "Sparrows. Not one falls without God willing it. And these birds here. On this page. I'm trying to find out what sort they are. I belong to a bird-watching club. We go out into the woods, looking for birds with binoculars."

"What birds have binoculars?"

"The birds don't, the bird watchers do."

"He didn't wave. My dad always waves when he goes somewhere."

Father Kelly said, "See that man there, how happy he looks? Well. That's how your daddy's going to look in Heaven. No more sickness. No more hard work at the hog plant. No more fields of stumps to pull. No more firewood to cut. No more worries. Eternal happiness with God in Heaven."

"Are there hog trucks in Heaven, Father?"

"And look over here." Father Kelly's finger pointed to a picture of a man and a woman sitting at a long table in a room with brick walls covered in vines. On the table was a loaf of bread and a roast of meat and dishes of grapes and bananas and apples.

"Do they have Cheerios and peanut butter in Heaven?"

"In Heaven, they have whatever you want."

"Are all the people Uncle Sam killed in Heaven too?"

"See how happy everyone looks? See that man there? That's what it's like in Heaven."

"Is that where wishes go, Father?"

Father Kelly leaned back and thought. "Probably. Yes. I think that is where wishes go."

"Are there wishing wells in Heaven, Father?"

Father Kelly closed the Bible and reached into his priest suit pocket.

"Can I get there with a ladder, Father?"

"Here's an envelope."

"He didn't pack any clothes."

"See there on the corner? That's the name of our church. Inside there's a blank piece of paper. I want you to write a letter to your father in Heaven. Like the Bible says. Our Father who art in Heaven. Rebecca will help. Tell him you're going to miss him but you're getting to be a big boy and you're going to help your mother and do well in school and grow up to be a person he will be proud to call his son, like God was proud to call Jesus his son. Bring the letter to the funeral."

"When he's finished up in Heaven, is he coming back like Jesus is coming back?"

"As soon as I find her, I'm hoping your Aunt Jeannie will come back. Won't that be nice? You won't remember your Aunt Jeannie. I knew her when she was your age."

"Are there bedbugs in Heaven?"

"Your Uncle Sam used to give out hymn books at church and your Aunt Jeannie sang in the choir. She had a lovely voice."

"Uncle Sam gave out hymn books?" asked Jiffy.

"He was a nice boy, the same as Leonard."

"Uncle Sam? A nice boy?"

In the middle of the night, I heard the back door open. Getting up and going to my bedroom window, I watched Ruth do her moonlight walk across the grass and up the lane to Pork Chop Road. But this time she kept on going, in the direction the ambulance had gone. She must have known my dad wasn't up in Heaven.

Then Jiffy came out, running to catch up with her to bring her back home.

SIXTEEN

Bobby

The next morning, me and Jiffy were sitting in the living room when Mr. and Mrs. Patterson and Father Kelly came over. Mrs. Patterson made us breakfast while Father Kelly showed us a picture taken one Christmas Eve at church twelve years ago. "Your Aunt Jeannie had come on the bus and stayed in the Queen's Hotel in Gore Bay until after New Year's."

He showed another picture. "She had long hair like yours, Rebecca, before you got it changed. It swung back and forth when she walked, and she always wore nice dresses. A lovely young lady."

Later that day, instead of Aunt Jeannie showing up, it was Uncle Ivan, dressed in work pants and a plaid shirt. He was almost as big as Mr. Patterson. The skin on his cheeks was lumpy like a toad and he had a straight-across mouth like a bullfrog.

While they talked about my dad falling off the tractor, Jiffy took me into the mud room and explained about Uncle Ivan's face. "The marks are from chickenpox. Uncle Sam told me. Uncle Ivan was in Vietnam with Uncle Sam, and then he was a used car salesman and then a window salesman, and then he had a job selling freezer meat. But none of it worked for him because the marks on his face scared people, which was good in Nam but not on Manitoulin Island."

Uncle Ivan and Uncle Sam were reading the insurance policy when we returned to the kitchen. Uncle Sam said, "In trust to Bobby. Here we got a million dollars sitting in an insurance company waiting for guess who to grow up?"

Uncle Sam pointed at me, sitting in the corner with my truck.

"In Nam kids his age are already working in the fields. Take that truck outside. You're getting dirt all over the place."

Jiffy took me upstairs. "The funeral is tomorrow. You have to finish your letter."

After Uncle Sam and Uncle Ivan left, we sat in the living room. Mr. Patterson sat in the chair that everyone sunk into like quicksand but not him. He sipped his cup of tea made by Jiffy while Mrs. Patterson read out loud my letter written in block printing with my grade one pencil. "Dear Death, when are you going to bring him back from Heaven? Did you get the wishes I sent? Do you know where the crowbar is? Yours truly, Bobby."

Mr. Patterson's cup of tea stopped halfway to his mouth. "Crowbar?"

"I think the letter should be to Dear Daddy," said Father Kelly. "Tell him you're going to be strong and help your mother — stepmother — and grow up to be someone she'll be proud of."

I started again, Jiffy helping, poking me, reminding me to say nothing about a crowbar in the letter. When I finished, I took it to Father Kelly, who was reading the insurance policy. He set it in his lap to read my letter. He read the words and said, "Good for you, Bobby," and then he sealed the envelope. But he ran his tongue back and forth across the glue too many times and too much spit came out. Some dropped on the papers in his lap.

"Bobby, give those legal papers to Jiffy," said Mrs. Patterson. "Tell her to put them away. She'll know where."

"She should know where," said Mr. Patterson. "She does everything else around here."

When I noticed the picture on the top corner of the insurance envelope, I showed Jiffy, who was at the sink washing the dishes. "See, it looks like an anchor, but if you hold it upside down it looks like two crowbars side by side, one this way, one that way, and right side up an anchor again."

Jiffy stamped her foot. "Bobby. Don't talk about crowbars. I told you."

Then she noticed that too much spit hadn't sealed my letter right. "Give it to me, Bobby."

Father Kelly, busy with Ruth in the living room, and the Pattersons gone somewhere, no one else watching, Jiffy slipped my letter out of the envelope. She said, "I'm adding something to what you wrote, Bobby. I know you have to tell someone, so let's do it now and then it's done. Here's what I'm going to write. 'I don't think it was an accident. When Bobby is eighteen, him and I are coming back for the crowbar. Then we're going to tell everyone what happened. Then everyone will know.'"

She slipped my letter into the envelope with the insurance policy and the will. Then she looked at me hard and whispered, "If there's no insurance policy, there's no money, and if there's no money, there's no Uncle Sam. He'll go away and leave us alone and my mother will sell the farm and we'll go back to Owen Sound and when you're eighteen you and I will come back for the crowbar and for these letters and for the money, which is yours."

She resealed the envelope. "Run your fingers along there, Bobby. Seal up your secret."

I did what she said.

She wrapped it in three Red and White plastic grocery bags. "We tie the open ends to seal up our secret." She tied the open ends. "There, Bobby. You told. Understand?"

I nodded.

"I'm not sure you do."

She opened a drawer and found a piece of string. "Tie it up. Loop the string around, like tying a shoelace, tied up tight, never to be opened until you turn eighteen."

Jiffy tucked the bag away in the kitchen cupboard. "Father Kelly is going to let you put your letter into the coffin. This is what you do.

At the funeral you put the bag into the coffin. The letter, the will, the insurance. If anyone asks why in a plastic bag, you say you don't want it to get dirty on the way to Heaven. No, don't say that. You can't say dirty at a funeral. Say something about clean. I want to keep it nice and clean for his long trip to Heaven."

"What's going to happen to us now?"

She sat on the floor. She folded up her knees and rested her head on her arms. "I don't know. Mylinh's coming back. I think Father Kelly will find Aunt Jeannie. She looks nice in her picture. She lives in a park in Toronto with no hog smell and no bedbugs and no stomach aches."

"What about your mother?"

"Dr. Brad has to look after my mother. I can't look after her. I can only look after you."

Jiffy stared off, the way she did when she figured things out. She said, "I'm going to tell you a story and I need you to listen. Remember that *Danny the Turtle* series? Remember how Danny hid in the grass peeking out from his shell? No one noticed him, but he noticed everyone and saw everyone's secrets. When anyone asked, 'Danny, did you see this or did you see this?' he said he was just a turtle hiding in the grass and didn't see anything. So that's what you have to be, like the turtle."

SEVENTEEN

Bobby

I was playing Danny the Turtle. From inside my shell in the kitchen corner, I watched Ruth at the table. Halfway through the lunch Jiffy made special for her, Ruth's elbows on the tabletop, her fork halfway to her mouth, her head halfway bowed, she stopped chewing and stared into her plate. I poked my head out of the shell and dragged myself one leg at a time, one, two, three, four, and tugged at the sleeve of the arm that held the fork. The food dropped onto the floor. Not turtle food, Kraft Dinner.

Mr. Patterson came back from Woolworths with a white shirt for me and a blue dress with blue stockings for Jiffy. Mrs. Patterson poked at the blankets until Ruth, who had left her plate of Kraft Dinner on the table and gone back upstairs, rolled herself out of bed. Mrs. Patterson helped her to get dressed. She rubbed red stuff on Ruth's cheeks.

Father Kelly came over. While we waited for Mrs. Patterson to finish with Ruth, Father Kelly told Mr. Patterson about the scratch on his car. "Looks like they took a key to it. I was in the Red and White grocery store and when I came out, there it was: a deep scratch all the way down one side. A little scratch I wouldn't worry about, but this was deep, down to the bare metal. I phoned Percy. He said some kid had done it. He's only a town policeman, not the OPP, but he dusted for fingerprints. You know with that powder and the little whisk because the insurance company wanted a police report. The insurance company said if they found the kids, the parents would have to pay the damage, about a hundred dollars."

I waited for Father Kelly to say, Bobby did it.

But Mr. Patterson said, "No one around here did it, that's for sure. One of those Gore Bay kids probably."

Mrs. Patterson rode in Father Kelly's car, and we rode in Mr. Patterson's car, Uncle Sam in front, me, Jiffy, and her mom in the back. But not Uncle Ivan, who had gone for Mylinh. The coffin sat at the front of the Little Current chapel, a jar of flowers at each end. Some people from the hog plant arrived and shook hands with Uncle Sam and me, and gave hugs to Ruth and Jiffy. They all seemed to know Uncle Sam from a long time ago at high school. They talked about Leonard who was a real worker and asked where was Jeannie. They remembered she worked for a while on the bacon line and then they went up to the front and looked down at Daddy in his coffin.

When everyone was sitting down, Father Kelly stood at the front and read from the Bible about ashes and dust and going to Heaven but nothing about eyes needing to be open or closed. If his eyes weren't closed when he was lying in bed, he wasn't dead. I hadn't gone up with my envelope yet, so I didn't know if his eyes were still open. He would need them open to find his way to Heaven in his coffin, the same as Mr. Patterson needed his eyes to be open to find his way to Owen Sound in his hog truck, the same as Uncle Sam needed his eyes to be open to see the bedbugs.

When Father Kelly finished, I went up to the front and asked could I put in the letter now. I explained about the plastic bag. When I went up to the coffin, I saw that my father's eyes were closed. I asked Father Kelly. He said, "God will show him the way."

On the way out of the chapel, Mrs. Patterson leaned over to Uncle Sam and said, "I've been meaning to ask you, other things more important, but what did you do to Jiffy's hair?"

"Her other hairstyle wasn't decent for going to church."

"Church! What's church got to do with it?"

Uncle Sam said, "From now on I'm going to be the one to take them to church and Jiffy has to look proper for her age."

Some church ladies came over so Mrs. Patterson couldn't say whatever she was thinking.

We followed the hearse. Little black flags fastened to the aerials of the cars ahead of us snapped in the wind. Some of them looked like rags by the time we reached the cemetery on the edge of town at the end of a gravel road. The cemetery looked like a field of square boulders thrown up by the frost and left to sit in the grass as green as early wheat. In the fields around the cemetery, the cattle-corn stood tall as me, almost as tall as Jiffy. Driving through the cemetery, Jiffy wiped at her eyes with a Kleenex. She put her arm around me. "Did you put the letter into the coffin?" She was leaning close, fussing with my new suit bought by Mrs. Patterson.

I nodded.

Jiffy rubbed at her eyes.

"His eyes were closed."

"They're supposed to be closed."

The stiff collar of my new white shirt rubbed against my neck and the tie was too tight and the shirt too hot. I watched ahead as the cemetery dust dulled the shiny black of the hearse. As we passed a statue of the crucified Jesus, Mr. Patterson crossed himself.

Uncle Sam took a long drink from his bottle of hawberry wine. "Last night I got down on my knees and I prayed to God. I asked him, Where were you, God, in Vietnam? Twelve-year-old Vietnamese girls squat down in the ditch, and you think they're having a piss, pardon the language, but then you look again and it's a baby they're having. They get up and leave it there to die and two days later they're back on the street hustling again."

"Now is not the time for war stories, Sam."

"If the captain came across one of these babies, he'd give it a poke with his boot to see if it was alive. If it was, he'd shoot it with his AK-47."

"There are children here, Sam," said Mr. Patterson. "Now is not the time for war stories."

"This isn't a war story. It's a God story. We dug holes and buried the babies because Charlie would booby trap the body to blow up whoever tried to pick it up. There was this one baby, I found it covered in bedbug bites, so I wanted to pick off the bedbugs and then put it with its mother who was under a pile of blankets in the doorway but Charlie was coming…"

"There are children here, Sam. They've just lost their father."

Uncle Sam tipped up his bottle. He wiped his mouth with the back of his hand and looked at the roof of the car. "So tell me, God, where were you when all this was goin' on?"

"Keep your stories to yourself, Sam."

"God's marines. God's on our side. That's how the Americans thought, and they had proof, they said. The proof is in the pudding, they said. But it wasn't pudding. It was nuoc mam, which was fish sauce that stunk worse than stale horse piss. Charlie put it on everything he ate, which was mostly rice and bamboo rats, so we always knew where Charlie was hiding. By the smell."

"Shut your mouth, Sam. Now is not the time."

From the back seat, I couldn't see much of Uncle Sam or Mr. Patterson except the backs of their heads and their shoulders and sometimes the sides of their faces. Mr. Patterson's suit jacket was twice as wide as Uncle Sam's. Uncle Sam was a marine and not afraid of anything but now in his narrow-shouldered suit, no baseball hat and no cigarette hanging from his lower lip, he didn't look much bigger than Jiffy.

"We'd crawl through the bamboo trees and elephant grass following the smell. I'd give the word and we'd stand up with our AK-47s blazing and wipe out the whole company. They never figured out that it was the fish sauce and I can't figure out now why the God that Father Kelly's been talking about would allow babies to die covered in bedbugs. To die clean like sacred like baptized like anointed with blessings and go to Heaven is one thing. But to die covered in bedbugs, Patterson?"

Uncle Sam wiped the marble eye with the back of his hand. "Were you in Nam, Patterson, defending our freedom?"

"Horse shit."

The two men stared at one another. Mr. Patterson's lips were tight, and the lines at the side of his mouth were like white scars. Like how they were when him and me sat on the porch step and took turns blowing through blades of grass pressed between our thumbs to see who could make the screechiest screech.

I hoped Uncle Sam would say, Well you can kiss my ass, Patterson. I looked over at Jiffy and I could tell she was hoping the same so that, what would happen, Mr. Patterson would stop the car and throw Uncle Sam over the fence where he'd land with a plunk in the cattle-corn.

But Mr. Patterson said, "We'll park here. That's them under the tree."

The grave was at the back of the cemetery in the corner beside a chain-link fence pushed almost over by a tree trunk. We got out of the car. Jiffy took my hand and led me over. "Don't sit in the grass, Bobby. You'll get stains on your new clothes."

I asked her, "Uncle Sam was the captain. Did he shoot that baby that had the bedbugs?"

"Yes, he did shoot a baby with bedbugs. In some place called My Lai where everyone was shot and the village burned to the ground. He told me one night when he was drunk. The reason he took a job as a gravedigger, he said, is because he's trying to bury that baby. There's something wrong with his brain from the war, like there was something wrong with Sarah's grandfather's brain from some other war. Different wars but the same brain disease. It's like Grandma said. You can see stuff without your eyes needing to be seeing."

When Jiffy said this, I looked over. Uncle Sam was too far away for me to see either eye but I remembered when he was looking for bedbugs I remembered when I looked up I sometimes saw a tear in the corner of the good eye that looked down at me and a tear in the corner of the marble eye that couldn't see me, as if, as it looked down, it was seeing some other me.

EIGHTEEN

Bobby

Everyone was standing around waiting for Uncle Ivan and Mylinh so they could unload the coffin and get started. When they arrived, Mylinh came over and gave me a hug. Uncle Ivan had a flask in one hand and a small black suitcase in the other. He went behind a tree for a pee. He came back, tucking his plaid shirt into his work pants.

Mrs. Patterson asked him, "What happened to Jeannie? She should be here by now."

Uncle Ivan took a sip from his flask. "Don't know, stuck at the ferry probably."

Uncle Sam took my hand and led me to the grave. "I dug it myself, with my backhoe." He pointed to it parked by the fence. "My partner said he'd do it but I said I wanted to do it myself. See how the sides are straight and the corners square? That way the coffin fits down nice and flat."

Uncle Sam squatted beside me. "We dug graves like this in Nam for witnesses. You know what a witness is, Bobby? Someone who sees something. Whatever you do, you got to make sure there ain't no witness left around to come back to bite you. See how flat the bottom of this grave is? No stones poking up to break through the wood and into the dead guy's bones. Talking about bones and stones, I was goin' through yer dad's tools and saw the crowbar's missing. It hangs inside the stable door." Uncle Sam squeezed my arm, his gold ring stabbing into my skin. "So when you find it and put it back, that's where you put it."

He stood. His fingers thin as bones took my hand and led me back to the others standing there, except Jiffy, off to one side with Mylinh, watching everyone like Danny the Turtle.

"What do you think, Father?" asked Uncle Sam. "Maybe that scratch on yer car didn't happen at the grocery store. Maybe it was at someone's house and that's when it happened. Did you check around? Maybe there are witnesses." He squeezed my hand.

"Too much willful vandalism by teenagers old enough to know better," said Father Kelly. "As it stands, the insurance pays. But where is the lesson in that?"

Uncle Sam said, "As far as I'm concerned, they should do a little jail time, you know, a week or two. You need to find a witness."

"Where's Jeannie?" asked Uncle Ivan, returning from another pee, this time against the fence post, not bothering about behind a tree.

"That question gets more tired each time it gets asked," said Mrs. Patterson. "She's probably not coming." Mrs. Patterson picked me up and hugged me. She carried me over to where Mr. Patterson stood by himself. She said, "No Jeannie. Who is going to provide for these children?"

Mr. Patterson said, "Leonard was the only decent one of the bunch, and even he wasn't much good at providing."

"We should phone Children's Aid. But I know if we do the kids will end up someplace worse, like Sarah Robinson and that little brother."

When Uncle Sam came over, Mrs. Patterson said, "Do we know what's going to happen with the children, Sam?" Mrs. Patterson's lips were tight, like when her cookies didn't turn out right. When an answer didn't come, and Uncle Sam looked off as though he hadn't heard her, she said to Mr. Patterson, "What do you think, Earl?"

Mr. Patterson stared at Jiffy's mom, who was standing next to the chain-link fence, almost in Uncle Ivan's pee. "Ruth is not capable, Sam. She shouldn't be on her own with two children."

Uncle Sam said, "Dr. Brad gave her new pills and now she's doing pretty good. She has her odd bad day but most days are pretty good. And Mylinh's gonna stay with them until Jeannie comes. Mylinh was already looking after them. Mylinh looked after loads of kids in Nam. Fifteen-years-old she went six hundred miles down the Mekong River in a rowboat with five kids and nothing to eat."

"And what is your role in all this going to be?"

"I'm the one who earns the money to feed everybody. You think it don't cost money to feed two kids?"

"And who was it decided to change Jiffy's hair?"

"Ruth did. It's more her age. Jiffy's hair was almost down to her waist."

"Bobby said Father Kelly told her it wasn't suitable for church."

Uncle Sam gave me a look. "Bobby's a little liar. He likes to make up stories."

Still no Aunt Jeannie so the funeral finally started. I stayed with Mrs. Patterson and Jiffy and Mylinh. Mr. Patterson and five other men came up to the coffin. He stood bigger than everyone in the cemetery, so big the bullets from Uncle Sam's AK-47 would bounce right off him. Mr. Patterson and Uncle Sam took one end and two from the hog plant the other end and two others in the middle. They set the coffin on straps over the grave to float there like a rowboat. First Uncle Ivan made a speech, sort of. He crouched down, talking directly to the coffin, his hand holding the handle so as not to let it drift off, talking to my dad as though he was in there listening, about how he always wanted to be independent and plant stuff and live off the land, so his dream had come true, sort of almost.

Father Kelly said a prayer and some other words that I didn't understand. And I didn't understand the signs he made, like writing in the air with his finger. Maybe he wrote some kind of special spirit note. When I pulled on Mrs. Patterson's sleeve and asked if that's what Father Kelly was doing, she said, "He's sending your daddy to Heaven."

"How is he going to get out of that coffin?"

Mrs. Patterson picked me up again. "Your father is still here with you, Bobby. He is in here." She put her hand on my chest. "He is in here." She put her hand on my forehead. "In your heart and in your memory. He will stay with you in your thoughts. Death comes and takes away the ones we love. But they are never gone. They feel close to us in spirit like they've only slipped into the next bedroom."

"Is that what Uncle Sam sees with the marble eye when he's looking for bedbugs?"

"There are no bedbugs."

"Will he write back an answer to my letter?"

"Where he has gone there is no real mail service. But he will always be there to answer you in your thoughts."

"Like in wishes?"

Mrs. Patterson nodded. "Like in wishes."

"Will he understand about what I told him?"

"He will understand what you told him."

Uncle Ivan and Jiffy came over. He set down his shiny black suitcase. "Father Kelly says we should wait fifteen more minutes before we lower the casket. So, I'll tell you what, Bobby." Ivan took a wristwatch from his pocket. He laid the watch on the palm of his hand. "You like this watch? I run a business of Swiss watches and knives. Import 'em direct from Switzerland. No store markup, no middleman. Bet you'd like to have a watch like this. What'll you give me for it?"

Ivan took a sip from his flask. With the back of his hand, he wiped away the beads of foam in the pockmarks around the corners of his mouth. "I paid factory price, twenty-five dollars for this watch. See this? That's an alarm. Tells you when to get up. Have a look."

I took the watch for a look before giving it back. The pockmarks looked like a disease.

"How old are you now, Bobby?"

"Six."

"Well, you're a good-looking kid. You got any girlfriends?" Ivan opened his shiny black briefcase that had been sitting next to his boot. It was full of watches, each one resting in a little holder. "How about a nice ladies' watch for your sister, Jiffy? Ten dollars for a twenty-five dollar watch."

Mrs. Patterson tapped him on the shoulder. "If you're trying to sell me watches for the kids, I'm not interested."

Ivan put the watch back into the case. He took another sip from his flask. He reached over to his case and folded a panel down over the watches to display a line of knives in black holders. "Maybe you know someone who wants to buy a Swiss army knife. See this one here? It's a collector. They don't make 'em like this anymore. This one here's a real army knife from Vietnam. I bought it off a guy. He had gold teeth. He was in Nam with me and Uncle Sam. We called him Teeth. He was short of money, see, but didn't want to sell his gold teeth so he asks me if I want to buy this knife so I say, 'How much, Teeth?' That's what we called him, because of his teeth. Teeth says thirty-five dollars. 'That's too much,' I say. 'I'll give you five for it.' So the teeth say okay. That's what it felt like when you're talking to him, like you're talking to teeth. So I bought one for Sam. See this here? For opening wine bottles. See this here? For cleaning fish. That's why these knives were good in Nam, for cleaning fish. You ever go fishing? Thirty-five dollar knife."

Mrs. Patterson said, "I might be able to give you five for a nice gold watch for Mylinh. Her birthday is coming up soon."

"You got five? Show me the five."

Mrs. Patterson opened her purse and showed him the five.

"Jesus," he said. "No kidding. A five. See that, Bobby? All right, it's a deal. For the five I'll give you the watch."

Uncle Ivan closed his case and headed off for another pee. Father Kelly came over.

"Jeannie is not coming, Father," said Mrs. Patterson.

"Well, I'm not sure…"

"Not sure is not an answer for the Jeannie problem. If you had a daughter, would you leave her with Sam? I don't think so. Standing around asking where is Jeannie is not solving anything. When Jeannie left, she said she would never come back as long as Sam is here."

"That was a long time ago, Emma."

"Jeannie hates Sam."

"We're not leaving them with Sam, we're leaving them with Mylinh to help Ruth."

"We already tried that once."

"And those pills worked pretty well. Until this happened, for the next two or three weeks, Ivan and Sam will be there to run the farm. And remember, we don't want to get the authorities involved because they'll send Mylinh back to Vietnam. She's been through enough, poor thing."

Mrs. Patterson said, "There is a reason why Jeannie has never returned and is still not here and that reason is Sam. Don't you get the picture, Father? The days of the happy island family with apple crisp in the kitchen and starched shirts in the bedroom closet are over. What's in the kitchen is a wine bottle. Ivan is drunk, in case you didn't notice, and who knows what's in Sam's bedroom closet … not starched shirts, that's for sure. So I'd rest easier if the kids stayed with me until Jeannie gets here."

I didn't hear what Father Kelly said. I was remembering my real mother made apple crisp in the fall, standing at the kitchen counter reading from a piece of paper how to make it, like Jiffy standing at the counter writing on my note and putting it into the envelope, which I had wedged between the fingers of his hands resting on his chest, one on top of the other, in the coffin.

So where was the envelope now? Was it in the coffin that they were lowering into that hole, or did he take it up to Heaven? And if he did, how could me and Jiffy come back for it when I turned eighteen?

I noticed the undertaker get into the hearse, start it up and drive along the cemetery road. I pulled away and ran after it, catching it at last. I jumped on the back bumper to look inside. Mrs. Patterson said my dad wasn't in the coffin. But he wasn't in the hearse either. Near the cemetery gate, I jumped off and stood in the grass by the roadside, watching the black hearse disappear into the dust spinning up in clouds behind it until it turned and was gone, leaving me there, watching the dust sink back to the ground. Father Kelly came over and said, "Your father's in Heaven with Jesus now and now it's time to go."

In the funeral chapel, Father Kelly had said some prayers about sending him to Jesus. But then, as everyone was leaving, before they closed the lid, when I put the envelope with the insurance and the will and the letter into the coffin, I saw he was still in there. Then, from the doorway of the chapel, I watched two men in black suits shut the coffin. Then from the back door of the funeral parlor, I watched them load the coffin into the hearse. I saw the coffin sitting there, him still in it, the lid shut tight, and still shut tight as he went down into that hole. So why were they saying he was up in Heaven?

When I saw Uncle Ivan kneel to talk to him, I knew. Uncle Ivan had figured it out too. My dad was still in there. He hadn't gone anywhere, except down into that hole, like down into a well.

NINETEEN

Rebecca

I was drawing pictures at the Pattersons' kitchen table; Bobby was outside with Mr. Patterson.

"Is Mylinh still over there looking after things, Jiffy?" asked Mrs. Patterson.

"Mylinh's gone to Toronto. Dr. Brad upped my mother's pills. She's doing pretty good now. She went to the Red and White and bought a bushel of apples to make apple crisp for Bobby and a carton of preserving jars to make her own strawberry jam to put down for the winter. And three new pairs of runners for me."

"Three? Why on earth three?"

"I don't know. They were on sale, I think."

"Is that a picture of a gun you're drawing?" asked Mrs. Patterson.

I turned the paper over and started again.

Mrs. Patterson asked, "Is that a picture of a barn?"

"It's our house," I explained. "That's the living room window and that's the kitchen window and that's my mother's bedroom window and that's Bobby's."

"Where's your bedroom, Jiffy?"

I examined the drawing. "I don't know."

"If Bobby's is there, yours must be here." Mrs. Patterson pointed at the spot.

"I forgot."

"Your house is the same as this house, except that you've got that mud room. Upstairs has three bedrooms, just like in this house. The front one your mother's and the next yours and the next Bobby's."

From my bedroom window, I could see the Pattersons' white frame house, and a little way down Pork Chop Road the next house, the Robinsons'. One Friday before the police took Sarah and her little brother away, me and Bobby had gone for a visit. We found the grandfather asleep in the drive shed. Then the police came for him. Then the police came for Sarah and her little brother. So now their bedrooms were empty.

"I'd like to see you draw the house again."

"I don't want to draw anymore." I set down the pencil and folded and tucked the papers away in my pocket. I went outside and sat on the step of the porch with Mr. Patterson and Bobby, who were sitting in lawn chairs. It started to drizzle. The drizzle turned to rain, drumming loudly on the overhang and gushing over the eaves to splash in the dirt. I found a dry place against the wall. I sat down, legs folded tight against my chest, to wait for the rain to end. I was thinking about Nellie who'd just had five pups. I was thinking about Aunt Jeannie, who still hadn't come. I was thinking about Uncle Sam not being able to pick up the baby and put it with the mother who was under a pile of blankets in the doorway of their hut.

My mind wandered across the lane, across the fields all the way to where Sarah used to live. Some other family without kids lived there now. On sunny days, a tall woman with her hair cut short would come out of the house to hang the washing on the line and then hurry back when it started to rain. In the sand by the clothesline pole, Sarah's little brother had sometimes played with his pail and shovel. One day, me and Bobby had gone over to play with Sarah who had one arm in a sling. Sarah wouldn't say how she hurt herself.

I asked, "Mr. Patterson? Where does Sarah live now?"

"I think in Regent Park in Toronto. But never mind about all that. Come and see what I've got in the garage."

Me and Bobby followed him through the rain along the lane, past their car, which was a new Buick, and into the garage.

"There's the cabinet I'm building. Don't tell Mrs. Patterson. It's going to be her Christmas present. There's still about six months so I should finish in time. The front doors open up like this, you see, with two shelves down and two up."

He pulled a box out from under the workbench. "Almost every little girl or boy who's come to visit on a rainy day has found something of interest in this old box."

Me and Bobby sat down with the box of toys: a car with a driver inside, a yo-yo with a long string, a badminton set with a net rolled up and tied with a ribbon. And three storybooks. And a doll with one eye blue and the other eye blank. The blank eye made the baby look like it had its eye on you, except it was looking somewhere else at someone else on a faraway television.

I hadn't thought much about television since we moved to the farm. I guess Leonard's back to the land didn't include television watching. Before my mother got sick, when we were living in that basement apartment, she'd say, "Turn off the television and get ready for supper," and I would turn off the television. Now she didn't care about a television. Or anything else.

Me and Bobby sorted through the toys until the rain ended. Hand in hand, we walked down the lane to the barn. Undoing the latch, I opened the stable door a crack and looked inside. Nothing in there but dust floating in the daylight running from the door to the hay piled in one corner. I stood looking back at the house, my right hand in my jacket pocket, my fingers feeling along the smooth surface of one of my drawings of Uncle Sam's AK-47. He'd brought it from his own farm and now he kept it in the stable of our farm. "To shoot any stray dogs that try to get into the chickens. Skunks, raccoons, stray dogs, whatever," he said.

My fingers found the paper I'd written my turtle story on. I had worked on it so long the paper was crinkled and smudged. I crossed the front line of stalls to the grain bin and found the storybook I had hidden. I brushed off the dust, tucked the paper into the storybook, and motioned Bobby to sit with me, so I could read it to him.

"One day Grandpa Turtle showed Danny Turtle how to walk on his hind legs."

I pointed to my drawing of the turtle's short pointy tail stuck out behind his shell, propping him up. "Next day Danny walked on his own, only two steps, but his grandfather laughed and clapped and did a turtle jig. Danny was so pleased with himself that he got right up again and walked to the end of the field. 'Only witness turtles can learn the art of hind-leg walking,' explained Grandpa Turtle. 'Now that you can stand upright, you can travel faster than other turtles, who usually don't go anywhere, except in the spring across the road. And now that you can stand upright, you can see farther than other turtles, who can see only what's in front of them. But with this blessing of hind-leg walking comes the curse of seeing. Normal turtles stay hidden in their houses out of sight in a nest of leaves and shadows in the forest undergrowth, or floating along down the river, only a tiny tip of the nose peeking out from the water, never seeing much of anything. But witness turtles can travel anywhere and see everywhere, sometimes witnessing what bad people do in secret.'"

I stopped reading. "What bad person did you witness do what bad thing?"

Bobby was studying the pictures, frowning, getting fidgety. "Is this a real story or are you making it up?"

"It's a real story."

Bobby pointed to a page in the book. "How come the pictures are different in the book?"

"You use your imagination."

"How come you're looking at those papers and not turning the pages in the book?"

I turned the page. "Danny was a curious turtle. With the gift of hind-leg walking, he travelled all over the country. When he found a spot he liked, he flopped out of sight in the green grass. He watched from his green shell, not moving an inch. He sat in the same spot for days, not even blinking his eyes. But sometimes seeing something far off, wondering what this might be, Danny stood up on his hind legs to see."

I stopped reading. "What did Danny the witness turtle see far off, Bobby?"

"I don't know."

I closed the book. "What did you see?"

"Uncle Sam…"

"Yes, but you can't tell anyone. If anyone asks, you say nothing." I stared stern as a school teacher at him until I thought he understood. "So what did you see?"

"Nothing."

"What do you know?"

"Nothing."

"Who are you?"

"Danny the Turtle."

"What did you see?"

"Nothing."

"If you see me with Uncle Sam's AK-47, what will you see?"

Bobby couldn't find an answer.

"Like Danny the Turtle. You see nothing. You tell nothing. You say nothing. I'm going to write a witness page in my diary where I ask you all the questions about Uncle Sam and the crowbar and then you put down your name and sign the bottom."

The stable door opened and Mr. Patterson called, "Jiffy? Are you in here?"

I leaped to my feet and returned the book to its hiding place.

"We're just playing, Mr. Patterson."

"Let's go down to the river," he suggested. "See the beaver dam."

We followed Mr. Patterson behind the barn, across a field stretched away to a line of trees that dipped into the ravine that separated the two farms. In the shadows at the bottom, the shallow river gurgled. For a while, me and Bobby tossed in sticks to watch them bob down the current and lodge against an old beaver dam: two logs covered with twigs and sticks jammed between two big willows. I threw in a piece of bark. It floated crossways to stop at the base of the dam next to a long upright stick covered with long-dead grass, standing like a thin man with a beard. Like Leonard. I broke up more pieces of bark and tossed them. Finally, feeling cold, I got up. The thick branches of the bushes grabbed at my bare legs as I took Bobby's hand and we climbed to the top of the ravine and stood beside Mr. Patterson, who sat on a stump watching us.

The sun had come out from behind a clump of trees where three cows watched a car racing along the gravel road, no dust swirling up in a cloud of smoke to drift across the fields because it had just rained.

"Mr. Patterson?" asked Bobby.

"It's Earl, big guy." He tousled Bobby's hair. "Call me Earl."

"Did Father Kelly get his car door fixed?"

"I don't know. I'm sure he did. Why do you ask?"

"Maybe there was a witness."

I poked him so hard he nearly fell over. "Your shoelace, Bobby. You have to learn to keep them tied up." I knelt to tie his shoelaces.

We went back towards the house.

Mr. Patterson said, "Lots of interesting things on a farm, lots to keep you occupied. When I was your age, we'd catch pigeons in the barn at night with flashlights. If you shine the light on them, they become paralyzed, you see. You can pick them right up and stick them in your coat. And talking about coats, Emma's got something for the two of you."

"Can we catch some?" asked Bobby.

"Maybe we can build a coop and get some homers," said Mr. Patterson. "But talking about homers, now is time for you two to go home after we go and see what Emma has bought for you."

"Goodbye," Mrs. Patterson called from the front porch as we left, Bobby wearing the new sweater and me the new red-and-blue jacket Mrs. Patterson had just bought for us at Woolworths.

My fingers found the paper I'd drawn the AK-47 on. If only I could do it without doing it. I put the paper in the pocket of the new jacket.

TWENTY

Bobby

Uncle Sam sat at the kitchen table drinking hawberry from the glass in his right hand and with his left hand smoking his Cignals. He held it between the first finger and the finger that had his gold ring that was as shiny as the barrel of the AK-47, which was resting across his knee.

Jiffy's mother was in bed and Jiffy had gone to the Pattersons'. Uncle Sam said, "It was a cloudy day in My Lai, like today, Bobby, and everyone in my troop wore themselves out looking for a crowbar and for letters from an insurance company. But we couldn't find 'em anywhere, so I figured one of them village kids took the crowbar and the insurance and hid them."

Uncle Sam sipped from his glass and dragged on his Cignals.

"So someone said, 'In that hut over there you'll find the boy with the letter and the crowbar.' I went into the hut. I was the corporal, see, and I dragged the boy out by the hair. He looked about yer age, Bobby. While I decided what to do with him, he stood with his head hanging, looking at the ground, like you're doing right now, Bobby. That's how I knew he'd done something wrong, his head hanging down like yers. He stood there, this skinny son of a bitch with his hair sticking up all over his head. He forgot to comb his hair, like you, and he wore a baggy old shirt hanging out of short pants that were all dirty and too big for him falling off his body, skinny as yers. Then his mother come out and threw her arms around him and screamed at me, 'Don't hurt him, he don't know nothing,' and then an old woman come out, the grandma probably, I don't know, they all look the same, Bobby, that was the problem. They all looked the same, they all wore this sort of shawl thing. She'd been in the hut, which up on stilts, and came down the wooden steps wearing army boots. I thought she was Charlie dressed like an old woman."

"I set my AK-47 into my shoulder. How was I supposed to know? They all looked the same. And I said, 'Where are the insurance letters and the crowbar?' Well, the boy, who looked about yer age, pretended not to understand English and not to know what I was talking about, like yer doing, Bobby. So I got pissed off. You know, Bobby, one way or the other, by Jeezus, the corporal gets what he wants. I pulled the trigger of my AK-47. I could feel the gun jarring against my shoulder, like this."

He held my arm and hammered my shoulder with his fist.

"When the gun stopped pounding against my arm, I see a big sister crumpled into rags on the ground and the little boy that knew where the letter and the crowbar was, he's lying on the ground. The old woman wearing army boots was still standing, but her eyes were empty, just kind of staring, and blood was pumping out of her neck onto this baby she had in this sort of shawl thing. I didn't know the baby was in there. I wouldn't have shot her if I'd known she'd had the baby in there but how was I supposed to know? She tried to pull it back into her shawl but it fell on its face in the dirt. The old woman was dead already but trying to get hold of the baby. She got hold of it finally by the arm, like this."

Uncle Sam took hold of my arm. "She turned the baby face up. Look at me, face up, Bobby. There was a bullet hole in her chest but no blood was pumping out. Then I see this baby is covered with red marks all over her body and then I see these little bugs, I was sure those little bugs were maggots and they'd already got started on the baby before I shot her so the baby was dead already and I hadn't shot her. But when I saw they were bedbugs I knew the baby was alive when I shot her. And then the blood started pumping out. Then I thought if I can get these bedbugs off her so they're not sucking away her blood she won't die. I tried to pick them off. I started picking them off. Then my buddy Teeth came over and said, 'Charlie's coming. Forget about the bedbugs. The baby's dead. They're all dead. There ain't no dead baby going to rise this day or any other day,' and while he was saying that the baby was looking up at me with big eyes that were blue grey brown, the same colour as my eyes. She was staring at me and me staring back into these eyes that kind of sunk away into a sort of fixed look of staring."

Uncle Sam's glass eye that was blue grey brown fastened itself on me in a fixed look of staring.

"But she did rise, Bobby. My first day here, sitting in this chair, I could hear the grandma's army boots clunking down that wooden slide thing one step at a time and when I turned to look I saw in your blue-grey-brown marble the baby's blue-grey-brown eye staring at me in a fixed look of staring."

Uncle Sam rubbed away the tear in the corner of the marble eye. His good eye in a fixed look of staring stared at the smoke coming from the end of the Cignals. With the back of his right hand, he wiped both eyes, both the baby's eye and the eye that could see.

He finished his glass of hawberry.

"I got to go over to my own place for a day or two. When I get back, I want that marble game gone, and that crowbar and that insurance letter back."

TWENTY-ONE

Bobby

I followed Jiffy and Mr. Patterson across the field to the river and then up the bank and across the bridge, and back along the path worn bare by her trips to the Pattersons'. A fly landed on my arm, crawled a few steps, then flew off, circled, and came back to land on my other arm. Sometimes, flies flew up in the clouds as I walked through the patches of sunlight on the barn floor, but this was the witness fly, and it flew along wherever I went.

"You want to see the puppies?"

As we walked along, Mr. Patterson snapped an apple in two, that's how strong his fingers were, and gave me half. Mr. Patterson took my hand. My hand shrunk in his big hand. We walked along, past Mr. Patterson's truck, its chrome wheels shining, past his new Buick, its chrome wheels shining. We went in through the big doors and across the bare board floor of the hayloft.

"When Nellie's not in the house, this is where she sleeps, in this old box. And this is where she decided to have her pups. No sense moving them into the house because she'd just move them back again."

Nellie's five pups were with their mother in a nest of towels Mrs. Patterson had fixed for her. Four were sleeping against her belly while the fifth, poking in the fur along her neck, tried to suck on the tag on Nellie's collar. "What is that?" I asked.

"A dog tag for identification. If Nellie gets lost, there's a number on the tag that tells who she belongs to."

"Like the tag Uncle Sam took off his buddy hanging off the fence?"

"Don't pay any attention to those war stories."

Mr. Patterson moved the pup to a nipple. Nellie lifted her head and thumped her tail two or three times, like saying thank you. As I stroked the soft nose of each, they stirred and yawned.

"Can I pick one up?"

Nellie watched me pick up the pure-white one.

"Can I take it home?"

"When the pups are this little, Bobby, they have to stay with their mother."

The pup began to cry and Nellie reached out with one paw.

"Better not handle them too much," said Mr. Patterson.

"Can I take this one outside?"

Mr. Patterson seemed not too sure.

"Please?"

"Maybe for a minute."

When we started away, Nellie got to her feet and trotted after us. But near the barn door, where dust floated in bars of light on the bare boards, she stopped, for the nest was crying for her to come back. We slipped outside and sat in the grass. I held the pup against my chest, stroking its soft coat. When it began to shiver, I tucked it under my sweater and curled around it to keep it warm. But cold nose searching across my bare stomach, it began to squirm and then cry so loud that I thought Nellie would hear.

"Time to go back to mother, I think."

Nellie's tail thump thumped thank you as the pup searched in the fur of her belly.

Back at the house, Mrs. Patterson hoisted me up onto the chair with the telephone book.

"I think he's too big for a telephone book. Aren't you, big guy?" Mr. Patterson took it away. "I phoned to ask your mother if you and Jiffy could stay for supper. She sounded fine today."

"Stew and dumplings," said Mrs. Patterson, "just the way we like it."

"And banana cream pie," added Jiffy. "I helped make it, didn't I, Mrs. Patterson?"

"You did indeed."

"And I cut the carrots for the stew."

"That too."

"Jiffy is a good little cook," Mrs. Patterson added.

I remembered how Jiffy's mom made apple crisp the week before, and how I brought some over to the Pattersons'. I said, "Remember? I said apple crisp was for picnics, so we pretended we were on one, and I made some Kool-Aid, remember?"

"How could I forget?"

Mrs. Patterson served the stew. While we ate dessert, I asked, "How many days until my birthday, Mr. Patterson?"

"Birthday! Not for a while." He looked at the calendar hanging by the clock. "About … a long time yet. Why? What did you want? We might not need to wait for your birthday."

"A new marble game. The one I've got sounds like army boots."

"I'm not sure if we can find one but we can try."

"Will you buy me a crowbar?"

"Crowbar?" asked Mrs. Patterson. "Why on earth would you want a crowbar?"

"To help Uncle Sam."

Jiffy kicked my foot.

"Can we build a fire in the fireplace?" I asked.

Jiffy gave me another kick.

But Mr. Patterson smiled. "Why not? If we can pretend we're on a picnic, we can pretend we're having a campfire."

While Jiffy helped Mrs. Patterson tidy the kitchen, Mr. Patterson showed me the right way to build a fire. "First the paper and then the kindling and then a medium piece and then the match."

With a hiss, the paper curled up and turned black. Smoke floated up the chimney and little points of red danced along the dry sticks. Inside the fire, yellow and blue flames sparkled like the coloured glass in Father Kelly's church windows; bits of gold sparked as the sticks grew into a roaring fire.

"Uncle Sam says the only way to get rid of bedbugs is to burn the house down."

"You're sitting too close, Bobby. You're going to burn yourself." Jiffy moved me away and then sat down beside me and poked me with her elbow.

"He plays with matches, Mr. Patterson. I think from watching Uncle Sam smoking his cigarettes. Next thing he's going to be rolling leaves up in paper and trying to smoke them."

"Boys will be boys. I remember—"

"Not when you were six years old you didn't," said Mrs. Patterson.

A yellow sheet of flame sprang up in front of me, grabbing at the dead branches sticking out like long fingers, turning them into clouds of smoke. When Mr. Patterson poked at the fire with his metal stick, and then closed the damper, the smoke narrowed into one single ribbon of grey like a thin man being snatched up the chimney and gone. Bye-bye, Uncle Sam.

"Can you help me dig up my dad?"

"Why would you want to dig up your dad?"

"The letter he put into the coffin," answered Jiffy, giving me the elbow. "He wants to change what he wrote."

That night at tuck-in Jiffy was angry. "You're not to tell. Don't say anything about that letter or about the crowbar. It's a secret. You are Danny the Turtle. You stay in your shell, and you don't say anything about what you saw or what you're going to see."

"What am I going to see?"

"I don't know yet." Jiffy sat on the bedside, her elbows resting on her knees, and stared into the floor. "But as long as Uncle Sam thinks you know where those papers are, you're safe. Safe, Bobby, except if you tell him."

"Can I tell Mr. Patterson?"

"No. Bobby. No, no, no. You aren't listening. He'll phone the police and they'll split us into foster care. Remember Sarah and her little brother?"

Jiffy pulled back the covers and climbed in beside me and pulled the blankets over our heads. "We're Danny the Turtle, hiding in his shell, watching everything, saying nothing."

TWENTY-TWO

Bobby

I was Danny the Turtle peeking out from the kitchen corner, watching what was going on. Uncle Sam and Uncle Ivan sat at the kitchen table drinking hawberry and smoking one Cignals after another. They talked about fighting the commies to keep everybody free. They said eighteen-thirty and twelve hundred instead of clock time. They didn't use grocery words like Kraft Dinner and Cheerios and peanut butter. They said C rations. Then Uncle Ivan made jokes about how in Nam the bedbugs were the size of cockroaches. The people living in the villages ground the bedbugs up to sprinkle on the fish sauce.

They talked about a buddy coming home and now he's afraid of thunder. They talked about a buddy who was burned alive. They talked about killing whatever was out there and then having a look and it's two little girls. They talked about that baby.

Uncle Sam said, "Her name was Khuyen. She'd be nine years old now, her hair in pigtails, from watching American television."

Then they talked about how the whole family lived in one hut and how ten-year-old girls slept with their uncles.

Uncle Sam said, "That's because more people in one bed means less bedbug bites for each person. You got to spread it around. You got two thousand bedbugs can live in your bed for one year on one bite so hardly anyone gets bit more than once. And they're not like beds. They're big mats on the floor."

Then Uncle Sam talked about how Aunt Jeannie didn't come for the funeral and never came to visit, except that one Christmas, and now she didn't come to help look after things. "If she don't come, she don't care and, by Jeezus, she ain't fit to be the guardian of these two little children. They need proper upbringing, church every Sunday, and decent clothes to wear to school."

Uncle Ivan took a pen from his shirt pocket and wrote on the back of his hand. When he showed it to Uncle Sam, I saw that it said $1,000,000, with a question mark after.

"I had the will and the mortgage in envelopes for when I went to the lawyer. Father Kelly was looking through them. He says he gave them to Bobby." He pointed. "To put into the cupboard. Now I can't find them and Bobby says he don't know where they are."

"Leonard's lawyer got a copy probably."

"He made out his own will, one of them forms, you know how he was, had to do everything his self. But how are we gonna contest the will when we don't have the papers?"

"Bobby's worth a million dollars." Uncle Ivan leaned back in his chair and lit another Cignals. "Why don't it go to Ruth?"

"They ain't married. Besides, she's nuts. If I got named guardian, they'd give me that million. That's why I need a lawyer. If there's no will, the estate gets frozen, like tied up, forever. But if we get that will, we can get it changed so the money goes to Bobby and to his guardian, me."

"Well, what about Jeannie?"

"Well, kiss my ass. What about Jeannie?"

"It should go to Ruth."

"What are you, drunk? Ruth is sick, nuts, whatever. The pills she got worked for a while but no more. Dr. Brad's gonna put her away. Then they should appoint me guardian so I get control of the money and use it…"

"Where is Ruth?"

"Upstairs. In bed. Where she always is."

"What about Jiffy?"

"Fuck me. What's the stupidest animal in the jungle? The polar bear. Jiffy needs lookin' after same as Bobby, so they appoint me."

"What about me?"

"What about you? I'm the one who's here doing all the work."

Uncle Ivan scratched at the marks on his face. He sucked on his Cignals. "If I was you, corporal, I'd walk away. Let the county look after them."

"Fuck sakes! Leonard's got a hundred acres of hardwood here. The big thing now on the mainland is to heat yer house with wood stoves. The Arabs can keep their oil. I already got contracts for the wood. I'm gonna make a bundle."

The next morning, I got out of bed and raised the blinds and watched Uncle Ivan climb into a hog plant buddy's car. I recognized the buddy from the funeral. They were leaving to deliver pork chops and Cignals to Mylinh's brothers' store in Toronto.

When I heard thunder, I looked up. Gone to Heaven, Father Kelly had said, pointing. But I couldn't see anything in those dark clouds that looked like those pictures of Heaven. Maybe first you had to find the door. But first he had to get out of that coffin.

I got my clothes on. But I couldn't find socks, so in bare feet, I padded to Ruth's bedroom. "Mommy," I said, pulling up the covers and climbing in. Usually, I didn't call her that. But with Daddy gone, I was missing my real mother. She rolled over and turned her back to me. Nests of black hair peeked out from her armpits as she pulled the covers over her head. I wanted to ask her, Will you make apple crisp, Mommy? But her smell, stirred up from under her blankets, changed my mind.

I went back to my room. I went to the window to look again. This time, I could see one cloud with a door in it. Heaven was probably through that door. Daddy's probably there by now. But he's left the door open. So maybe he's coming back.

I heard Uncle Sam's brand new Mr. Safety boots clump up the stairs and along the hall to Jiffy's bedroom. I heard the bed squeak and heard muffled voices. I snuck along the hall to peek in. Jiffy was sitting on the edge of the bed. When Uncle Sam sat down beside her, she flopped back and rolled away. I ran to my room and in a minute, Jiffy came in and closed the door and climbed into my bed.

At night, when she tucked me in, standing over me, Jiffy looked big and brave, like Mr. Patterson. When she reminded me about my shoelaces, she was like Mrs. Patterson. When she held my hand and walked with me along the school hallway, she was like a teacher. Now, curled up in my bed wearing those pigtails, she was like a little kid, more like my age.

I said, "I'm hungry."

"Wait till he goes," she said in a little kid's voice. "We'll go to Mrs. Patterson's for pancakes."

"Mr. Patterson likes pancakes. He says, doesn't matter how flat you make them, they still have two sides."

Jiffy didn't answer. She just held on to me tight. About an hour later, Uncle Sam called us out. He stood in the long grass beside his pickup, one shoulder higher than the other because the bad leg was sore because of the new Mr. Safety boots. I smelled the hawberry on his breath and saw the red lines in his marble eye.

"I'll be back in an hour," he said to Jiffy. "Bobby says he put the will in the cupboard but it's not there. So where is it? There's gonna be trouble around here if it don't turn up soon."

He reached into his shirt pocket for his lighter and his Cignals. "Feels like rain coming. The wind's changing." He sniffed at it. "They're making bacon today. Good. Viet needs more bacon."

He took one Cignals and tapped the end a few times on the face of the package before putting it in his mouth. With the thumb of his right hand, he flipped open the top of the lighter and spun the wheel. As he cupped his hands against the wind and brought them up to light the cigarette, the flame glinted on the gold ring with the blue stone.

Uncle Sam climbed into his pickup. His dust boiled up the lane and down the gravel of Pork Chop Road.

"I've got a stomach ache, Bobby. I'm going to bed. You go without me to the Pattersons'."

I knew she wasn't going to bed. With Uncle Sam gone, she would go into the stable and bring out the AK-47 and sit on the old milking stool she'd wiped clean so as not to get her dress dirty. The AK-47 had a bolt that slipped out and a little chamber for the bullet. But when she pulled the trigger, nothing happened.

I followed the path to the Pattersons'.

"How is your mother doing, Bobby?" Mr. Patterson sat down for his coffee and pancakes.

"She won't get out of bed."

Mr. Patterson's elbows were on the table. In his hands, his cup looked like a baby cup, or like one from a dollhouse set. Underneath him, the chair looked like a baby chair.

I thought Mrs. Patterson would say, Earl, take your elbows off the table. Instead, she said, "Is Mylinh there, Bobby?"

I shook my head no. I poured maple syrup onto my pancakes.

"Why isn't she there?"

I stopped eating and stared down at my pancakes, round like the shell of Danny the Turtle.

Mr. Patterson was waiting for an answer. Finally, he said, "You finish your pancakes and then go on home, Bobby. I've got a doctor's appointment for my heart and then I'm going over."

I gobbled my pancakes so I could hurry home in time to watch Mr. Patterson's car pull up the lane and stop where Father Kelly usually parked. So I could watch Mr. Patterson come up the path. He didn't walk like Father Kelly who took short steps like Jiffy's mother, and he didn't limp like Uncle Sam, one shoulder higher than the other. He leaned himself forward in solid steps, his hog boots planting themselves flat in the dirt. His eyes scowled at the house the way he sized up a pen of pigs, singling out the boss hog to load first so the others would follow up the ramp, into the truck, and off to the slaughterhouse.

TWENTY-THREE

Rebecca

I knew that if Mrs. Patterson was the one coming across the porch and into the kitchen to ask the questions, no matter what I said, Mrs. Patterson would have read in my eyes what I was feeling and thinking and seeing, the signs plain as the words in my diary wedged in the stone wall of the well.

But it was Mr. Patterson.

"Uncle Sam's gone on deliveries, Mr. Patterson. He said he'd be back in an hour. But that always means three."

"Are you sure he's not around somewhere?"

"I think he went to get frozen meat. Uncle Ivan is in the freezer meat business."

"And your mother?"

"She's upstairs."

"How is she doing?"

"She was feeling better two days ago. Bobby asked her this morning to make apple crisp, so maybe she will."

He looked at me, his face full of questions, looking for signs of anything not right.

"Would you like some apple crisp? If she makes some, she'll make enough for a whole army."

"Army? Have Sam and Ivan been telling you war stories?"

"Just … she sometimes makes too much."

He drew in a breath. His chest heaved up in such a big sigh I thought his shirt would split. "Emma makes apple crisp. One of my favourites."

The word "army" had slipped out, not because of war stories, but because I had been watching Uncle Sam sitting at the kitchen table peeling an apple with his army knife. While he ate his apple, he polished his AK-47 the way they taught him in the army, by Jeezus, sliding out the bolt, sighting along the rifling, oiling the stock, wiping down the barrel, sliding in the bolt, putting on the safety. I knew the bullets were on a shelf above the grain bin with .22 calibre written on the box. I could have taken Mr. Patterson right to them, shown him how to slip in the shell and jam it into the chamber with the heel of his hand. Then I would ask him: How do I release the safety? Then, if he asked, Why do you want to know that, I'd tell him. And that would have been the end of Uncle Sam.

What I needed to do with an AK-47, Mr. Patterson would have done with his bare hands. Arms big enough to hoist a four-hundred-pound hog into the slaughterhouse could dump Uncle Sam head first down the well, squealing and squirming like the pig he was.

Mr. Patterson opened the door to leave. "Apple crisp," he said. "Bobby's favourite."

In my diary, I wrote that it was the apple crisp, him and Bobby's favourite dessert, that turned Mr. Patterson around. It was the mention of apple crisp, the thought of it baking in the oven, that turned him around and sent him home. If there had been no apple crisp, he'd have waited for Uncle Sam, stayed there on the porch sitting on the top step, the AK-47 across his knee, and when Uncle Sam returned, shot him. Together, Mr. Patterson and me would have disappeared Uncle Sam under those tree roots and he would stay disappeared like Mrs. Patterson's disappeared children. They wouldn't find him for a hundred years, like that dead boy they discovered when they dug up Pork Chop Road, his skull clean and smooth as Mrs. Patterson's white teapot, with no clues left for how he got there. Then I would show Mr. Patterson the Witness page in my diary where I asked Bobby all the questions about Uncle Sam killing Leonard. Then I would show Mr. Patterson the Witness page in my diary where I had copied down what Bobby had told me about the crowbar, all of it in my best writing with the dates and the times and Bobby's signature at the bottom, everything recorded.

I saw in Mr. Patterson's eyes how the mention of apple crisp changed his mind and saved Uncle Sam's life, bad for me, but good for Mr. Patterson. Bad and good. Sometimes all it takes is one word to change everything and turn everything in a different direction, not the one you want but the one you have to take. Bad and good I made a choice, me not Mr. Patterson.

But then, at the door, he stopped. "I nearly forgot. Lend me your flashlight." From the pocket of his overalls, he brought out a magnifying glass. "Let me have a look." He went upstairs.

I went out and sat on the porch step and waited.

I heard Mr. Patterson's boots come up behind me. He was holding the magnifying glass in his left hand. In the palm of his right hand were tiny reddish bugs no bigger than apple seeds. He said, "These aren't bedbugs or hayberry bugs. They're baby cockroaches. Bobby's been eating in bed and they've got a nest in his mattress. When they get bigger they'll move to the kitchen. Tell Sam to get some traps."

I sat on the porch and listened to the early September wind rippling through the tall cattle-corn, turning brown now, the breeze from the river always colder than the one from the hog plant, two different winds depending on which direction they were coming from, north or south, like my mother, bad days or good days, like me, bad choices, good choices, depending on which direction the mind was coming from.

Load Uncle Sam into the wheelbarrow, Mr. Patterson. Wheel him across the field and dump him into those tree roots, bye-bye Uncle Sam. Now you know how it feels to have knots like tree roots so twisted around your stomach that you can't eat Mrs. Patterson's pancakes.

Time for breakfast, Jiffy, Mr. Patterson would say. Smell those pancakes.

Hand in hand, Bobby and I would follow Mr. Patterson from the pups in the hayloft to the butter and maple syrup in the kitchen.

A deaf-mute girl in my grade four class at school had trouble telling me what she was thinking and feeling and seeing but that didn't matter because I always knew from reading her eyes every time she looked up after trying to tell me with her hands.

What did I see every time I looked up: the dead cigarette smoke stuck to the ceiling, the hog smell hanging in the air, the fist of aches in my stomach. What did Uncle Sam see every time he looked down: the dead baby lying in the mud, the dead buddy hanging off the fence, the dead men, women, kids, dogs, cats, goats he machine gunned from his Cobra.

TWENTY-FOUR

Bobby

I followed the path to the Pattersons'.

"Come in, Bobby. Have a chair. How is school? Pretty good? My goodness, you're getting thin."

"Is Mr. Patterson here?"

"He's in the barn."

I got up.

"You're shaking, Bobby. What's the matter? You sick?"

I shook my head.

"How is Ruth, Bobby?"

"She's sick."

"I thought she was doing better again. I thought everything was back to okay. I thought she got new pills."

"She did but she gets them mixed up."

"Then someone needs to give them to her."

"Uncle Sam gives them to her."

"Uncle Sam? Not Jiffy?"

"Jiffy gets stomach aches."

Mrs. Patterson put on the kettle. "I heard gunfire a while ago. Rabbit hunters, I guess." She opened the cupboard over the sink and took out the tea bags. "I was about to make my two o'clock cup of tea. Would you like a glass of milk?"

"Yes, please."

"Who's looking after things? Is Mylinh there?"

"No."

Mrs. Patterson brought me a glass of milk. She asked, "You sure you're not sick?"

I nodded.

"How come you're shivering then?"

"Jiffy says Mr. Patterson should come."

"Bobby." She took my truck off the table and put it on the floor. "That day Mr. Patterson went over. He'd just been to the doctor. Mr. Patterson has a bad heart and high blood pressure, the same as your grandma. I told him to stay out of it, especially now that your mother was up and around and doing fine. She even came over to thank me for all the help. She gave me a dish of apple crisp. She was all cleaned up with a nice smile. Thank God, I said. They've got her on the right medication."

"Jiffy says he has to come."

Mrs. Patterson sighed. She wiped her hands on her apron, then took it off. "Let me have my cup of tea first."

***

Mrs. Patterson came over. She waved her arms at the stove. When she opened the oven door, smoke filled the kitchen. She grabbed the oven mitts and pulled out the pan of apple crisp and carried it outside and set it in the grass. She sat down opposite Jiffy's mother, sitting bent over at the kitchen table in pajamas and bathrobe, staring into a half-finished plate of Kraft Dinner, her hair flattened at the back from lying in bed.

Mrs. Patterson laid the oven mitts on the table. "What is wrong with this picture, Ruth?"

Startled, Ruth jumped. "What? What picture?"

"Where is Jiffy?"

"She says she has a stomach ache. She's in bed."

Mrs. Patterson followed me up the stairs, careful not to trip on the broken step. We found Jiffy under the covers.

"What's this about stomach aches?"

"We don't have any money."

"I thought Father Kelly and Dr. Brad were working with the insurance company to get money."

"It won't give us any."

"Show me your mother's pills, Jiffy."

Jiffy pulled herself out of bed. She was wearing a sweater over her heavy winter Miss Judy's shirt from Woolworths. While she was getting the pills, Mrs. Patterson sat on the edge of the bed and stared at the floor.

Jiffy handed them over.

"I thought the doctor took her off lithium. And what are all these other pills?"

"These are left over from Grandma and this is her nitro and these three are leftover lithium from before. Uncle Sam gives her the lithium."

Mrs. Patterson went over the window to read the labels on the three bottles.

"He gives her one of each," said Jiffy.

"But these are all the same, lithium with different dates. One of each but not all three together. What did Dr. Brad say he should give her?"

"I don't know."

Mrs. Patterson led the way down the stairs.

"What is the matter with this picture, Ruth?" She put the pills on the table in front of her.

"What picture?" Ruth looked around.

"Go into the bathroom and get cleaned up."

Ruth pushed herself from her chair and shuffled her way to the kitchen sink. She turned on the tap, but rather than washing her hands or her face she stared at the water sliding down the drain.

"Why is Sam giving you all this lithium, Ruth?"

Jiffy said, "She had full bottles left. He wants to use them up so they don't go to waste."

Mrs. Patterson sank down into Uncle Sam's chair. "God help us. He's sicker than she is." She shoved the Kraft Dinner into the centre of the table. "I'm going to ask Dr. Brad about this. Put one lithium back but I'm taking the other two. If Sam says anything, tell him I threw them away."

Mrs. Patterson scraped the Kraft Dinner into the garbage. "If you're going to stand there, Ruth, you can wash the plate. Let me see you wash the plate."

Ruth put the stopper in the sink, opened the cupboard door, and brought out the soap.

"Earl calls it Raft Dinner. It tastes like ground-up logs, he says. Wash the plate and then you go up to the bathroom and get cleaned up proper."

When Jiffy's mom returned from the bathroom, I saw that she had combed her hair but her eyes were still puffy. Mrs. Patterson took Ruth's hand and sat her at the table. "Ruth, what's happening when you're not looking after Bobby? That's Bobby I'm talking about, the one sitting right there. And do you know what Sam is up to? Maybe nothing, I don't know, but it's your responsibility to know these things."

"Jiffy looks after everything," Ruth said.

"Jiffy looks after Bobby, but no one looks after Jiffy. She's too young, not yet ten. It's too much responsibility. Come upstairs and we'll get you dressed."

They went upstairs.

I put on my warmer coat and played with my truck in the ditch by the fence. Around supper time, the wind shifted and the hog smell came back and Mrs. Patterson came out. I watched her disappear along Pork Chop Road, a ribbon of brown between the black trees and the grey sky where the black crow flapped, rising above the hog smell to a black dot disappearing, maybe gone for the winter, like the heat-bugs that used to whistle in the trees, gone for the winter, and the grasshoppers that used to jump in the afternoon sunshine at my feet, gone for the winter, and like the witness fly, disappeared, gone for the winter.

Because of the broken wheel, my truck didn't work right. It tipped over when I hauled it along the gravel lane. Leaving it, I climbed out of the ditch and went along the lane and around behind the barn to sit on the tractor, its flat tires half buried in dead goldenrod. From there, I could see Ruth's bedroom window, the blinds down and the curtains pulled. If she wasn't in bed with the covers over her head, she stood at the window staring out, waiting for Leonard to come home from work.

After I had got tired of sitting on the tractor, I waded through the grass to the well. If I leaned over and looked down, I could not see the water. But I knew it was there, and I knew that was where Jiffy was going to put Uncle Sam after he got accidentally shot by a rabbit hunter. The hole under the tree is too far, she'd said. And if we throw him into the hole, we got to fill it with dirt, but it's too hard to dig. If we throw him down the well, all we have to do is push the stones in after him. Disappeared forever, like Mrs. Patterson's children.

I sat in the grass and listened to the whispers coming from the cornstalks Uncle Sam had planted in the field beyond the lane. High above me, the crow that I thought had gone for the winter floated down to sit on the fence post. It sniffed back and forth at the hog plant smell, then lifted itself into the trees where Uncle Sam and my dad had cut the firewood that was piled in the mud room now, with more stacked by the chicken house. No more buying oil from them crazy Arabs, they can kiss my ass, by Jeezus.

TWENTY-FIVE

Bobby

Dr. Brad came over with the right pills. Father Kelly brought Mylinh back from her brothers'. She moved some of her clothes from Uncle Sam's farm so she could stay until Ruth's new pills made her feel better. Mylinh cooked the rice in the well water, which tasted okay with lots of ketchup. She asked about the wishing well. I told her. The wind takes the wishes from the clouds to float through a door in the sky into Heaven. Every wish is like a teeny white feather and all the feathers together make up a cloud. Some days there are lots of people making wishes so some days there are lots of clouds. Those are white clouds. Black clouds are bad wishes. If you wish bad wishes they don't go to Heaven. They come down when it rains and mix in with the hog smell and turn everything to mud. Then the water from the mud goes underground into the well and that is why it sometimes tastes bad.

Mylinh understood. She explained why Uncle Sam woke up at three o'clock in the morning and couldn't get back to sleep. "Because my dead relatives are there, staring at him from the end of the bed. First, they sneak into his bedroom and stand at the foot of his bed to make sure he's sleeping and then they climb into his bed. He will wake up at three o'clock in the morning and he will look and he will think it's my grandmother staring at him, wanting to get into his bed."

I asked, "What will your grandmother say?"

"She won't say words but she will make Uncle Sam think about the bad things he did."

"If it's a baby what will it say?

"Babies talk with their eyes. If you want to know what the baby is saying you look into its eyes."

"Like Uncle Sam's baby."

"In My Lai where my whole family was shot and the whole village burned to the ground."

I expected her to say, That baby was my sister. I waited for her to say it. It was like that witness fly was whispering in my ear, Uncle Sam shot her baby sister.

But she said, "I have both my arms and both my legs and I'm not getting shot at anymore and my brothers have a whole store full of good food. But Uncle Sam has so many dead bodies coming to stare at him in the night and tell him things he shouldn't have done that he would need to be in bed all day and night to keep up so mostly he doesn't go to bed. He wanders around, talking to his dead buddies. Except when he's here, with you and Jiffy and the Agent Orange."

Mylinh went back to stirring her rice. Then she said, "No one knows who shot who. But what I know is, with the disability money he got from the U.S. government, Uncle Sam brought me and Viet and Willie Billy over here. He set Viet and Willie Billy up with that store and gave me a place to live until I get my papers."

***

Every day Mylinh phoned Viet and Willie Billy in Toronto. She had a sing-song voice when she talked to Viet, but she talked to Willie Billy like he was in grade one. The sunlight through the kitchen window put sparkles in Mylinh's long black hair when she kneeled to wash the kitchen floor. Jiffy was trying to teach Mylinh to read and write in

English, but she was having a hard time learning the alphabet. After every lesson, Jiffy would say, "Write down the alphabet." Then she would say, "Write down all the words you can spell." Mylinh could write only two: "Coca Cola."

Mylinh knew how to sew and wanted to make curtains. Mrs. Patterson brought over the material, a different colour for each window. Jiffy's had to be pink, and mine blue. Mrs. Patterson offered her sewing machine but Mylinh did it by hand. Her and Jiffy sat at the kitchen table with needles and thread. The curtain rods should be hollow for hiding money, Mylinh said, and the curtains should be fireproof. But Mrs. Patterson said don't worry about that, this is Canada.

Mylinh hummed to herself while she cooked and cleaned. Until, when the weather turned colder, she had to light the wood stove. She was afraid of fire from when they burned her village down, maybe to kill those bedbugs that were really cockroaches. So, if Jiffy wasn't there, she would clatter the iron door and drop the wood on the floor and make as much racket as she could to wake Ruth, who sometimes lit the stove but usually didn't.

Then, one day, Mylinh left. Viet needed someone to look after the store for a day or two. Then it turned colder. Then the hog smell turned to entrails. Pulling the coat collar tight around my neck, I sat with my back against the cold iron stove and watched the first snow drift past the window. I heard Jiffy's steps on the back porch.

"It's freezing in here," she said, feeling the stove. "There's wood right here. Where is Mylinh?"

"She had to go back to the convenience store."

Jiffy was kneeling beside the stove, scrunching the paper. She stopped. I waited for her to add the kindling.

"When is she coming back?"

"I don't know."

She took my hand and we went upstairs to the bedroom. "Mother, you let the fire go out again. You know where the wood is. I left it there for you."

Dressed in the same clothes day and night, her eyes puffy, hair not combed, flattened at the back, Ruth stared at Jiffy.

"It's me, Jiffy. This is Bobby. I don't think you're taking your pills the way you're supposed to. Don't take them from Uncle Sam. Take them from me."

From the mud room, Jiffy brought more kindling and two chunks of wood. After placing it all in the stove, the paper first, then the kindling and then the wood, she took the matches from the top shelf of the cupboard where the pills were and she lit the fire. Dancing red flames jumped out of the hole in the top as she put on the lid.

"Come over here with me, Bobby, by the stove."

Jiffy opened the draft at the front and pulled a kitchen chair close. I climbed up on her knee and she set my truck on the floor. She wrapped her arms around me. Through the five round holes in the black door of the stove, I watched red and yellow shapes snap like Uncle Sam's AK-47 in the flames.

"When are you going to shoot Uncle Sam and dump him down the well?"

"I don't know." Jiffy said this the way she would say it's time for bed or time to feed the chickens. Finally she said, "I have a pledge I want you to sign."

"What's a pledge?"

"A promise that can't be broken."

"Why do I have to sign it?"

She rested her chin on the top of my head. After a while, as the stove crackled and the room warmed up, she took out a paper and a pen. She read what she had written.

Jiffy had a little lamb
Whose laces were untied.
Everywhere that Jiffy went
The laces they did drag.
Then one day the lamb got lost
And Jiffy tried to find

Searching for his shoelace trail
Surely left behind.
The years went by and time did pass
The lamb grew big and strong
For Jiffy's little lamb
Had grown into a ram
Who followed now her shoelace trail
Until he reached its bend.
And then he saw his sister, Jiffy
Waiting at the end.

I looked out at the snow drifting past the window. I felt the heat from her body warm against my back and felt the heat from the fire warm on my face.

"It's our pledge. Bobby. I want you to sign."

I signed where she pointed.

"I'm bigger now, Bobby, but soon you will be bigger. Mrs. Patterson says you're going to be bigger than Daddy Leonard. I'm going to disappear. But I want you to promise to come for me when you get big. That's why I wrote the poem. That's why I asked you to sign it."

"Where will you be?"

"I can't tell you. But if I don't kill him, he'll kill you because you're a witness who won't tell him but might tell someone. If you tell, Uncle Sam goes to jail, yes I know that, except then you and I get separated into foster care. But if I kill him, I can wheelbarrow him to the well, and dump him down. They'll spend forever looking for him and for me. Meanwhile the Pattersons' will look after you. They won't let you go to foster care if they think I'm still alive and will come back for you."

TWENTY-SIX

Rebecca

I don't know who called him, but he came. Dr. Brad drove up the lane in his four-wheel drive Cherokee. He did not knock on the door but walked straight in. His questions were written on his face. I pointed. Without taking off his coat and hat, he opened the door to upstairs and thumped up the steps, me following.

"Get out of bed, Ruth. Sit down over here in this chair so we can talk."

She pulled the covers over her head.

He pulled them off. "Get up, Ruth."

She sat up, thin as wire now, the clothes she'd been wearing for three days creased into wrinkles. Dr. Brad stood at the bedside, scowling down at this skinny woman in her heap of smelly blankets.

"What's the use," he said.

I followed him back down. Dr. Brad set each foot carefully on the stairs, watching for the broken step. "How come it's so cold up there?"

"We only got one stove. It only heats downstairs."

"Don't you have a furnace?"

"The furnace doesn't work. We heat with a wood stove."

"Why don't you have electric heaters then?"

"We don't have any. Just the wood stove."

He took off his hat, one like the men wore in Mrs. Patterson's old England movies. He glanced about the kitchen: the linoleum worn bare from the sink to the table, the walls yellowed from smoke, a patch of crumbling plaster along one wall and ceiling where the roof leaked. He looked over at Bobby sitting in the corner with his truck.

Dr. Brad sat at the kitchen table. "Okay, Jiffy. What have we got that makes sense? I'm putting Ruth in the hospital in Espanola, which means you need a permanent caregiver of some sort. In a case like this, Children's Aid is called in but our Children's Aid works according to the law. What happened to Sarah and her little brother, I mean, we don't want that to happen to you and Bobby. All this you know. The will we can't find, which means the insurance money and the farm ownership will be tangled in government probate, which will take forever. So here is what is being done: Father Kelly has arranged a loan through the church for money to be used for groceries and such. Mrs. Patterson will look after giving out the money. Mylinh has agreed to live with you and Bobby long term, with no more trips to Toronto. If she follows through, she gets her papers; if not we send her back to Vietnam. Strong words but she needs to understand how the system works here."

"Uncle Sam's been giving her too many pills."

"She's had so many different prescriptions, pills all over the place probably, he couldn't keep track. That's why I'm putting her into the hospital, first to get the meds balanced again and then get her health back. The family court judge is a fishing buddy of mine. I explained your mother's condition is manageable providing she takes her medication the way she's supposed to. She had three repeats on her lithium and kept on taking it after I took her off. Plus, she was taking the Valium, which is a bad mix. As soon as her health is stabilized, she'll be back home. Mrs. Patterson will keep the pills and bring them over each day. I know what you're thinking, Jiffy. Here we go again. I'm blaming some of the problems on me for not keeping track of her pills better. I'm an old-fashioned country doctor, not a psychiatrist.

I've already done enough damage without putting you and Bobby into foster care. In the meantime…"

He stood to take off his coat.

"In the meantime, how are you doing, Jiffy?" He sat at the table. "Tell me what your day looks like. You go to school, I know, but what else? And what about Bobby?"

"Usually Bobby goes too, but he was sick today."

"Come over here, Bobby. Let me have a look at you."

Dr. Brad felt along Bobby's throat, pulled back his eyelid, and looked into each eye. "Stick out your tongue, Bobby." Dr. Brad placed his hand on Bobby's forehead. "Not eating enough, it looks like. I'll see how he is after he gets a few decent meals into him. Now you, Jiffy. Emma says you get stomach aches. Let's have a look."

I flinched when he lifted the bottom of the sweater to poke at my stomach. "Your appendix is okay." He felt my forehead. He looked into my ears with a chrome tube thing. "Everything seems okay," he said. But when he looked into my eyes, and I looked into his, I could see that he didn't believe anything was okay.

He took my hand and held it in both of his. "You're a brave girl, Jiffy, capable of looking after everything, I bet. But this is too much. You can't be here on your own. Mylinh must be here every day. We do things kind of different on the island, bend the rules to look after one another. Mylinh will stay. There is nothing more important to her than citizenship. That is the deal we made to get her back here. All she has to do is stay here with you, and I will give her my recommendation and so will Father Kelly and so will the family court judge. We look after our own."

He took my other hand. His fingers weren't thick and rough like Mr. Patterson's, or calloused like Uncle Sam's. They were warm and gentle, like his eyes.

"Is there anything you need to tell me, Jiffy? Anything happening here that doesn't seem right?"

When I hesitated, I saw Dr. Brad's eyes change. I felt the questions he was putting together cross the space between him and me and come through the wall that I had grown around myself. I felt the tears in every word of the answer I wanted to give come up from the knots in my stomach and into my eyes that were already giving to Dr. Brad the answer without me saying any words.

"Don't be afraid, Jiffy. I'm here to help."

It's Uncle Sam, I almost said. Every room in this house is filled with the walled-in closed-door smell of him, worse than the hog plant.

Dr. Brad reached out one finger to dry the line of tears running down my cheek. I knew he was reading the words written in my eyes, and I knew he knew I was ready to put them into sentences, even write them down and sign my name that what I said was true, like I did with Bobby, the witness. I thought of each letter of the word Witness in my diary, how I'd printed the W and the I and the T and the N and the E and the S and the S on the top of the page. I imagined him reading my signed statement. I imagined his long pauses as he listened to each of my silent words turn themselves into a voice so strong I could watch it open the closed kitchen door and cross the porch to get Mr. Patterson. Then I could see him coming, his hog boots thumping across the porch and into the kitchen, his big hands balling into fists that laid Uncle Sam on the floor, his glass eye popping out of smashed cheekbones to lie there looking up at me as my foot came down and smashed it to pieces.

"Tell me, Jiffy. Is it Sam? He's a bit rough, I know, but this is a farm, and you need a man on the property to keep things running. A lot of men came back from Nam a bit rough. It seems to take them a while to reintegrate. Most deal with their feelings by not talking about them, by keeping them inside. Sam is the opposite. He is not the type to bury his feelings. He acts them out. He talks constantly to give his feelings words but most of what he says never happened. There are four Viet vets here on the island and Father Kelly has started a group in the church basement, which Sam has joined."

"Uncle Sam joined a group in the church basement?"

"For counselling. Reintegrating into normal life."

He waited.

"Now is the time. Speak to me, Jiffy."

"Uncle Sam joined a church group in the basement?"

"And Father Kelly says Sam is going to start taking you and Bobby to church."

"To church?"

"Rebecca. Let me call you Rebecca. What is it that you need tell me?"

"The smell," I said finally.

"What about the smell, Rebecca?" Dr. Brad leaned forward to wipe along each cheek with a gauze bandage he had found in his doctor bag, because now that I could not give him the words, I could not stop the tears the words were coming from.

I wanted to say, the smell, the bedbugs, the shadow, the stomach aches, the smoke. They wake me up at night. First, they suck all the air from the room, and then they suck all the air from my lungs and then they suck all the air from me.

I caught myself before the words like the tears got away on me. "But I think that's the wood stove. The wood is too green. It doesn't burn right."

"What else?"

"The smoke stings my eyes."

He sat back in his chair to sort through what I'd said. I saw he had tears in his eyes too. I thought, if he wipes them away, he will see and then he will know. He looked away and blinked the tears away. When he came back, he hesitated. I knew he was going to guess, and I knew I would not be able to answer with another lie.

But he said, "First thing tomorrow we'll get the furnace fixed or get some electric heaters, although this is all old wiring so we have to be careful. But we've got money for that and volunteers from the church to do the work."

Dr. Brad stood to put on his coat. He hesitated. He sat down. He seemed unable to leave. He leaned over a little, searching my face.

"Rebecca? Anything else?"

I shook my head.

Dr. Brad seemed to be thinking he could go and should not go, both at the same time. Finally, he put on his hat and went to the door. I watched him cross the yard and climb into his Cherokee and drive off. A little while later the same men that took away Leonard laid my mother on the same gurney and took her away in the same ambulance.

The next day Mrs. Patterson asked me to go shopping with her. She bought toilet paper, cans of stew, cans of vegetables, jars of fruit, no peanut butter; healthy-looking cereal, no Cheerios. When we got back to her house, she put on the kettle. She showed me her new teapot. "This will one day be yours, Rebecca," she said. "With a pot like this, you pour in the hot water, be careful you don't scald yourself, and swish it around to warm it up. And here is the new tea cozy."

She sat down to wait for the tea to steep. "God works in mysterious ways, Jiffy. We never had children of our own, but I think He had a plan and that plan was you and Bobby. I don't know what Dr. Brad told you, but I have connections through Child Find. I have spent my life helping others and now it's time those others helped me. Be patient, Jiffy. Don't give up hope. I think it's all going to work out. We promised Dr. Brad we'd keep a close eye on you for the winter. The community looks after its own children; we don't send them away somewhere. We don't want that to happen again. I told Dr. Brad not to tell anyone, but we're making inquiries of our own, Earl and I, to see what we can put in place. We wouldn't be able to adopt you and Bobby because we're too old, but something might be worked out. We have to be patient."

I said, "Uncle Sam has joined a church group in the basement."

"I know, Jiffy. But he's one of our Canadian boys who ended up victims of the American war machine just like our Indigenous children ended up victims of the Catholic Foster Care machine. They all need our help."

After tea, she began to sort the groceries. "Look at that. I've bought too much toilet paper. And these cans of stew I'll never use. And all these vegetables. You might as well take them home. Show Mylinh these cans of stew. Tell her I bought too much stuff. No sense throwing it away. She might as well cook this instead of rice. That's what you tell Uncle Sam, if he asks. He's not going to like charity."

But that is what we're getting, I wanted to say. That is the arrangement. So why are we pretending? Uncle Sam in a church group? Uncle Sam taking us to church?

That night, when I put Bobby to bed, he asked, "Who told Dr. Brad to come?"

"I don't know. It doesn't matter. I'm not changing my mind."

I tucked him in and turned out the light.

***

I was in bed listening in the dark to the wind howling outside my window. The electric heaters were on and the house was warm top to bottom. Mylinh had cleaned the kitchen with Grandma's vinegar mix and scrubbed the bathtub and sink. Two men from the church had fixed the leaky taps and the broken step and two ladies from the church had tidied the living room and the bedrooms. Mylinh couldn't figure out the proper temperature of the new second-hand electric stove from Nick's Appliance in Gore Bay. So, the burned cookies covered the hog smell.

Bobby's teacher came by with some homework to help him get caught up at school. She was a square-block-looking woman in a navy-blue suit with padded shoulders, her grey hair pulled back in a bun and covered with a hat that looked like a helmet. I served tea with the not-so-burned cookies. I showed her Bobby's room and mine. Mylinh stayed in the kitchen, probably afraid of a woman who looked like she belonged in the army.

"These Vietnamese girls are a marvel," said the teacher. "They're using them a lot for childcare. They're so happy to be someplace safe with enough to eat and money left over to send home. They don't care about the long hours."

The teacher said that my mother should be back in two weeks when her medications got balanced. "It's the drug companies, making these chemicals that mess up people's brains. The worst thing you can do when you're feeling down is to lie down. Get up and get busy. So they give you drugs that make you so dopey all you can do is lie down and do nothing."

Then she asked me if I had anything I wanted to tell her.

When Dr. Brad had asked the questions, he had been wearing an ordinary plaid shirt and ordinary pants. He looked like he was going to the river to catch minnows, but instead of carrying a tin pail, he was carrying his doctor's bag. He had set it aside and set his doctor voice aside and he set himself in the chair. He looked like a neighbour the way Mr. Patterson was a neighbour, which is why I almost told him.

But the teacher was dressed in a navy-blue suit from the U.S. army. She looked mean and had a hard voice. She didn't look like anyone you'd tell secrets to or go to the river with. So, when she asked the exact same questions, my mind traced backwards one by one to each of the letters of each of her words, but I could hear no concern in her alphabet of sounds and therefore could feel no tears wanting to come up from my alphabet of feelings that had almost got turned into words for Dr. Brad.

"We're doing fine."

"Are you sure, Jiffy?"

I looked over at Bobby who was watching us from under his eyelashes. "Bobby is getting tired of eating rice."

I wrote in my diary it looks like everyone except me has joined this let's pretend church group in the basement.

TWENTY-SEVEN

Bobby

For every day that Jiffy did not kill Uncle Sam, he grew bigger. Sometimes, as the step, thump, step, thump of his Mr. Safety boots clumped by my bedroom door, I could feel his bigness coming through the walls. Each morning, when he stood at the bathroom sink in only his work pants, I saw the hair that covered his back and chest was getting thicker and blacker.

"Dr. Brad phoned to say Ruth would be back in a day or two," Uncle Sam said to Mrs. Patterson when she dropped by. "And Mylinh is doing fine with the children. Mylinh is here every single day, no more trips to Toronto. I go twice a week to my church group. And we got new baseboard heaters installed for when Mylinh don't want to light the stove. Father Kelly comes by every Sunday to take the kids to church."

The snow that came had melted but there were no leaves left on the apple tree. The sparrows flew from one dead perch to the next, sometimes into the bare bushes standing like sticks along one side of the house. Uncle Sam bought twenty more laying hens and another champion Rhode Island rooster. Uncle Ivan set up freezers in the basement to store the pork chops and roasts he got from Teeth who was now supervisor at the hog plant shipping and receiving.

Every morning after the roosters crowed, Uncle Sam went to work at the Little Current Cemetery. "Lots of work," he said. "Lots of old people dying. That's how you can tell it's gonna be a hard winter."

Uncle Sam took out one cigarette and tapped the end a few times on the face of the package before putting it in his mouth. With the thumb of his right hand, he flipped open the top of the lighter and spun the wheel. As he cupped his hands against the wind and brought them up to light the cigarette, the flame glinted on the gold ring with the blue stone.

"The same ring as the pope wears on his finger, Bobby. Me and the pope got the same ring. The pope is a buddy of mine."

Uncle Sam slipped the ring off his finger.

"See there? On the inside? It says, Pope Sam Jones. The pope made me honourary pope for killing all them commies. The pope's a buddy of God in Heaven. I asked the pope to ask God to ask yer daddy in Heaven where that will is and where that insurance policy is and where that crowbar is and then ask God what he thinks I should do to the kid that hid them on me. God knows everything. So guess what the pope said, Bobby? He said you're a church-going man now, Sam. You've put the past behind you and now all that's most important to you is those two children. So why don't you pray to God yourself and ask Him direct. And guess what God said, Bobby. God said he'd ask your daddy. And guess what your daddy said? He said, I get lonely up here in Heaven and I've been meaning to ask if you, since you're God and can do anything, if you could bring Nellie up here for company. So God said, Why not trade with Bobby — the papers and the crowbar for Nellie. But I said no way, not Nellie. She's Bobby's. God said, and those papers and that crowbar are yours, Uncle Sam, so either you get the papers or Nellie comes up here to Heaven. That's what God said. If you don't believe me, ask Father Kelly next time he comes."

That Saturday morning Tug Wilson arrived with boxes of Cignals in the trunk of his car. He had thick lips and hair black as Mylinh's, and almost as long as Jiffy's used to be, and a honker of a nose like in the picture on the cigarette package. That same Saturday afternoon Mylinh's brothers came from Toronto for the cigarettes and the pork chops and the roasts. The fat brother with black eyes peering out of a fat face was called Viet because his last name was Nhan. His English was better than Mylinh's. He told Jiffy he'd heard so much about her and was glad to finally meet her. He had something wrong with his feet so every so often he'd take off his shoes and rub his toes, which were yellow and curled like a chicken's. Uncle Sam said he'd stepped on a mine in the war. The second brother, Willie Billy, was little and skinny and not much bigger than Jiffy. He smoked Player's one after another in a silver holder so he could suck right down to the filter. The smoke from his Player's smelled different than from Uncle Sam's Cignals, the same way smoke from the wood stove smelled different than the smoke from burned cookies.

Willie Billy followed Viet wherever he went and sat on his haunches to rub his toes when Viet did. Willie Billy's eyes followed Jiffy wherever she went. Between puffs, he said, "Jiffy make Willie Billy good wife someday."

"There ain't nothing wrong with Willie Billy's toes," said Uncle Sam. "It's his mind that don't work right. He's seen too many skulls on bamboo sticks. But there ain't nothing wrong with his willy."

Two more people drove up the lane. Uncle Ivan and a lady called Verna who looked like she was made from cement blocks.

Verna said, "My husband, Stew, was in Nam with Sam. I was a waitress in Stew's restaurant. When he told me he had cancer, he said if I married him he'd give me the restaurant when he died. Last summer, he died."

Verna had a daughter, Carly, about Jiffy's age. Verna said Jiffy could come to Toronto and hang out with her daughter anytime. Verna talked about the fresh air and heaved her chest up and down to suck it in. "Have you got any fresh eggs I can buy? But not if the hens are mixed in with that new rooster."

There was no room for all the pork chops and the roasts and the cigarettes and the eggs and the people in two cars, so on Sunday me and Jiffy went to Toronto with Uncle Sam to deliver the rest in the pickup. We went first to Viet and Willie Billy's and then to Verna's. They all lived next to the train tracks in old brick houses with the front part changed into the store part. Viet's was called Geary Convenience because it was on the corner of Geary Street and Dufferin. Down the street, Verna lived behind her restaurant called Stew's Lunch.

We stood in sunshine in Viet's narrow backyard by the train track fence. First, we heard the whistle and then the screech and then out of a tunnel came the train, rattling along the tracks and disappearing into another tunnel.

"Those are spiral tunnels," explained Uncle Sam, coming out to say time to go in twenty minutes. "We used to shortcut through the train tunnels in Nam, hopping every other sleeper like hopping rocks in a river bed. There wasn't no ventilating system, so we had to wet down rags and hold 'em over our noses and mouth so we didn't choke to death on the fumes or get poisoned from the water dripping off the tunnel's roof. If I want to go to Stew's house, instead of going all the way around by Dufferin Street, I climb the fence and hop the sleepers through the tunnel. The train runs every thirty minutes so I have lots of time to make a two-minute trip."

Uncle Sam left to do business at the insurance company. Jiffy and Carly went off somewhere. Viet and Willie Billy and me and Verna sat by the tracks and listened to Uncle Ivan's war stories.

"What regiment was Stew in, Verna?" Ivan took a sip from his flask.

"I don't know. The twenty-third maybe."

"Couldn't have been the twenty-third. The twenty-fifth maybe."

"It was the twenty-fifth then."

"I knew all those boys in the twenty-fifth. I fought alongside all those boys. See this here?" Ivan pulled up his pant leg. "Blew it off with a mine, damn near lost 'em both. Feel it."

"Feel it yourself."

"Go ahead. It's wood. Put your hand up inside my pant leg and feel it."

"Feel your own leg."

Ivan laughed. He pulled his pant leg back down. "Stew was the cook. Cookie, they called him, because he was a cook. He kept his head shaved bald so he didn't have to wear one of them cook hats. He didn't make nothing but commie stew. His name was Stew and all he ever made was stew but we called him Cookie even though he never made any cookies. He had a big stew pot mounted on the back of a truck with a little platform near the top so he could get up there and stir it with a big wooden ladle. As we marched along, he'd be up there, stirring his commie stew."

Uncle Ivan sipped from his flask.

Verna said, "Stew was not the cook. He fought the commies same as you."

"Early in the morning, we'd been taking sniper fire."

"He wasn't a cook, and he wasn't bald. His name was Stew, not Cookie."

"But by ten o'clock, everything was quiet and peaceful and by lunch, the sun was out and it was nice and warm so we all sat down in the grass to eat our lunch. But no one could find Cookie. They looked all over for him but couldn't find him nowhere. So they got out the plates and served themselves. 'Where's Cookie?' everyone said as they ate up Cookie's stew. 'This is the best stew he's ever made. He must have added something.' He'd been out on the roadside picking up leaves and stuff. He knew all about adding leaves to give stuff flavour."

"You're making this up. That was some kind of convoy. There weren't no convoys in Vietnam. And they never marched."

"Well," continued Ivan, "they finished up the stew and washed up and put away the plates, and then Sam climbed up to turn off the fire under the stew pot. As he was fastening down the lid so it wouldn't fall off while they were going along, he noticed what was left of the commie he'd shot out of the tree about on hour back was lying at the bottom of the stew pot. So that's how his stew got the name commie stew."

"You're making this up. Stew wasn't a cook in the war."

"You're right. I'm pulling your leg, feel it, put your hand in here. Big Bob, I call him." Ivan finished the last of his flask. "You know why

I'm not offering you a drink? I don't drink with no one who ain't a vet. If he ain't a vet, then he don't need to drink. Them guys who fought in Vietnam and got their legs blew off, they're the ones who need to drink."

"Your leg probably got run over by a truck."

Ivan laughed and lit a cigarette.

When Uncle Sam got back, he said, "As soon as the insurance company checks a few things out, they're gonna release the funs one month at a time 'til Ruth gets back on her feet…"

"It's not *funs*, it's *funds*," said Verna. "And where is Jeannie, by the way?"

"Living in Regent Park now."

"Regent Park, doing what?"

"Doing nothing. Collecting welfare."

Uncle Sam lit a Cignals.

"What's welfare?" asked Jiffy.

"Free money from the government," said Uncle Sam. "Like free money from the insurance company. Time to go."

I didn't know if he used the free money he got from the insurance or the money he got from selling the cigarettes and the pork chops and the roasts to buy his new van. Not the eggs. He gave those to Verna for nothing. Jiffy and me watched him load the empty boxes into his new van. Afraid I would scratch the shiny black paint, I backed away from the side of the van and stood next to Jiffy. I could see myself in the reflection of the smoked windows. I could see in the smoked windows the look on Jiffy's face. I think my look might have been the same look I had on my face when I scratched Father Kelly's car. But for sure Jiffy's look was the same as when she was sliding back the bolt of the AK-47. And when she glanced over at Carly who was standing off waving goodbye, I for sure knew where Jiffy would hide after she shot Uncle Sam.

TWENTY-EIGHT

Rebecca

Dear Diary: Mrs. Patterson asked me what my stomach aches mean. What I want to say is I don't know what anything means. My feelings are a jumble of alphabet letters I can't put into words. I see Uncle Sam and he speaks nice words learned in his church group, but I don't know what they mean. Listening to him and Uncle Ivan talk about the men in the church group I think they all brought home from the bogs and the swamps of Vietnam the bugs they couldn't burn or bury. Maybe for Uncle Sam its worse because with only one eye it must feel like looking at the bugs through the wrong end of a telescope.

Dear Diary. In Mrs. Patterson's dictionary I look up the words Uncle Sam is learning in his church group: trauma, cognitions disorder, hallucinations, rage, shame, all of it caused by your head full of carnage, another name for rape, torture, mutilation. And what you smelled burning was your brain on fire from the dioxin in the Agent Orange that the U.S. military kept dropping on you by mistake. So Mrs. Patterson would say, before Nam they had good well water in their buckets, but it got filled with bad bog water from the Vietnam swamps. So now down the well their farm bucket goes and up from the well a Nam bucket comes. But according to the therapy person, all that's happening is the hog plant smell of burning entrail triggers Agent Orange triggers trauma triggers the nighttime bedbugs that come back to bite them in their sleep.

Dear Diary: Uncle Ivan says that what the therapy person says won't make no sense to anyone that wasn't a vet. The therapy person says everyone has bedbugs that bite in the night but the Nam bugs are the size of cockroaches.

Dear Diary: Ruth thought the pills would save her from her bedbugs, like Leonard thought fresh air would save him from his bedbugs, like I thought Mr. Patterson would save me from my bedbugs, like Uncle Sam thinks the church group will save him from his bedbugs.

Dear Diary: I was telling Mrs. Patterson that when Grandma wasn't cleaning and scrubbing, she sat in her chair and knit scarves for the bad winter she could see coming. Mine were pink wool because that was my colour. Leonard's were blue wool because that was his colour. Bobby's were blue like Daddy Leonard's. For Uncle Sam she knit no scarf. What colour could she give him? The smudge her thumb was trying to wipe off the coffee cup was so it would be clean for when the church group gave him a colour.

Dear Diary: Without his marble game — Uncle Sam burned it in the wood stove — Bobby sits and makes shadows into bedbug shapes with his hand. He doesn't talk to anyone. Just plays with the shadows and shapes he makes with his hand. When I asked Uncle Sam why he burned the marble game he said because the marbles dropping down step by step came back like army boots to bite him in the night. After he told me that, sometimes I would catch myself, and I would look at my hands and realize that I was sitting making shadows into bedbug shapes with my hand. I'm sure that therapy person would say, all that's happened is the bedbugs that Uncle Sam brought with him to your house that first day he arrived have gone first to Bobby's bed and are now in your bed.

TWENTY-NINE

Bobby

Friday after school, me and Jiffy followed the path across the field to the Pattersons'. Mrs. Patterson sat Jiffy in the kitchen chair to take the pigtails out of her hair. "Your natural hair is beautiful. You don't need to do anything — let it grow down to your waist. Tell Uncle Sam you want it long and straight." Mrs. Patterson set down the brush and used two baby robin barrettes she bought at Woolworths to hold the hair away from Jiffy's face.

Last spring, we found a real robin sitting in the grass by the wishing well, waiting there for Jiffy to kneel and pick it up. When she did, it started to squawk and flap, it was so happy that Jiffy was going to look after it, which she did until it got big enough to fly away.

Mrs. Patterson said, "Father Kelly says there's a hold up with the insurance money. Something about the accident. Did he tell you?"

"He hasn't been by," said Jiffy. "There's been a lot of funerals at the graveyard."

"But Mylinh is there?"

"I'm teaching her English. She thinks hot dogs are made from dogs. Uncle Sam says in Vietnam you can eat your own dog, but not other people's unless it comes on your property."

Saturday morning Nellie sat in our lane. I got a slice of bread from the kitchen. She didn't want to play the toad game because she was looking for her last pup, given away the week before to Father Kelly, who was a lonely priest and needed company. From feeding her litter, Nellie had got thin and was always hungry. She lay on her belly, holding her treat between front paws, gulping it down in two mouthfuls. The following day she sat in the yard by the porch. As soon as I appeared on the step, she got up and wagged herself forward and stretched out her nose to smell the baloney. She had nearly reached my hand when Uncle Sam came from the barn and threw a stone at her. She hobbled across the field and disappeared.

"That dog's gonna get at my chickens."

Early next morning, Sunday, when I raised the blind of my bedroom window, I saw Nellie sitting in the lane looking at the house, waiting for me. I pulled on my shirt and sweater and jeans and running shoes and a coat. When I came out on the porch she jumped up, wagging her tail, happy to see me. But then Uncle Sam stepped out from the barn with his AK-47. Nellie slunk away. Halfway down the lane, she stopped and looked back. She sat down.

Uncle Sam came up on the porch with his rifle across his shoulder. "I was a sniper in the war. When you've got the person in your sights, even when they can't see you, and you're about as far as here to Nellie, that last second before you pull the trigger, they turn and look at you."

Uncle Sam tipped back his baseball hat. He brought the AK-47 to his shoulder and sighted on the dog. "The insurance is asking questions. Tell me where the crowbar is and I won't send her to Heaven to live with God."

I knew he wouldn't shoot Nellie. Nobody would shoot Nellie. Then the rifle snapped and the shot pinged off the gravel and Nellie jumped to one side. She crept forward, stretching out her nose to the spot the way she did when she found a toad.

"Where is it, Bobby?" He slipped in another bullet.

When Nellie sat down instead of running away, I shouted, "Run, Nellie! Run!"

The rifle snapped and Nellie jumped a three-legged hop and wheeled around as the second shot pinged off the gravel at her feet.

"Run, Nellie!" I waved my arms and stamped my feet.

But Nellie could only limp, her head bobbing at each step down the lane. A second before Uncle Sam pulled the trigger the third time, Nellie turned to look. She somersaulted one complete turn and crashed in a heap on the gravel. She flattened herself out straight, all but the bent leg. She began to twitch and then she relaxed and shrank a little smaller and sank flatter into the grass and lay still.

"Well, kiss my bald ass," said Uncle Sam. "I didn't mean to do that. But that's what happens, Bobby. If I don't get that crowbar back, something worse is gonna happen."

Uncle Sam took me by the arm and hauled me over to the dog. "In the military, you follow orders. If the corporal says this is what you saw, then that is what you saw. Maybe along comes the general and he says, 'What did you see?' What you saw was what the corporal said you saw. Anyone says different, gets shot like this dog. What happened to yer daddy, he fell off the tractor and banged his head. That's what you saw."

Uncle Sam knelt beside the dog. "See this shot? Nice and clean, like a hole in a board after you pull the nail out. Can't hardly see it. Not like that crowbar, which is easy to see. Have you seen it, Bobby?"

I shook my head.

"Anyone who lies to the corporal gets shot like this dog. Maybe if you went looking for it, you might find it. Maybe you did something with it you shouldn't have, like this dog doing something it shouldn't have, like trespassing on our property to kill my chickens. It's too late for this dog to undo what she did, but it's not too late for you to undo what you did. Wherever you put it, it's not too late to bring it back."

Uncle Sam stood. "The insurance company is asking questions. If they don't like the answers, there is no money and we starve."

He poked at Nellie with his foot. "Take it down to the river, the crows'll eat her."

He took the AK-47 inside.

I sat in the laneway gravel staring at Nellie who looked like a fur coat thrown down. Then she looked like something wrapped in a woolly blanket, like the baby Uncle Sam shot. I crept closer. I could see the little red hole darkening the fur of her neck. Because of the way she fell, her head twisted over her shoulder, one brown eye looked up at me as if she thought I did it. I nudged one front paw with my shoe. Then I sat on my heels, wondering how to get her to the river.

Uncle Sam came back. "What's the matter? Afraid she'll bite?" Uncle Sam picked up Nellie by the hind leg. "Take it down to the river."

When I grasped one front paw, not the broken one, Uncle Sam let go and Nellie crumpled at my feet. I started down the lane, dragging her to the path that crossed the field and dropped down in a curve to the river. I left her in a heap on the bank near the bridge.

I began to shiver. There was no sun and the November gusts along the river blew cold. Without looking back, I followed the riverbed under the iron bridge, picking up dry leaves and twigs and bits of grass as I walked. I laid these out in the black gravel basin under the bridge the way Mr. Patterson had shown me. I laid on some half-burned sticks from my last fire. Because wind blew in through the narrow part under the bridge, I had to lie down and curl around the basin, sheltering the match with my body. The flames sprang up in orange and blue, climbing up the black concrete, lighting up the shadows between the iron beams above me. I could feel the cold rush of the river move over to let in the heat, warming my face and arms and legs. After a few minutes, the concrete had warmed up enough that I could sit with my back against it and feel the warmth. The wood snapped and the sparks floated through the air to the river's edge where the current gurgled over the stones. The gurgle of the water made me shiver. I piled on more sticks and soon my crying was drowned out by the crack of the flames in the roof of the bridge. Eyes closed, I leaned into the heat, listening to the wood snapping like rifle shots in the fire.

"Bobby! Who lit this fire? Did you do this?" Jiffy grabbed my arm, pulling me away. "You're not to play down here."

"Uncle Sam sent me."

"Not to light fires he didn't." She bent down to brush the dirt off my pants. "It's bad to light fires. What's going to happen if you do?"

"I might burn something."

"Burn something is right." Taking my hand, she started up the path.

"He shot Nellie."

"Nellie? Is that what he told you?"

"I wouldn't tell him where you hid the crowbar so he shot Nellie."

"It wasn't Nellie. Show me. No one would shoot Nellie. Not even him. Show me. Some other dog who looked like Nellie."

But by the time we were halfway to the spot where Nellie was lying, Jiffy was crying, walking ahead of me so fast I had to run to keep up. I began to think, Maybe Nellie wasn't dead after all. She was sleeping. Coming along the river bank, I saw her, lying there still, like sleeping.

Jiffy looked down at her the way she did when she found the baby robin. I waited for Nellie to wake up and wag and lick Jiffy's hands and face when she kneeled and picked her up. Jiffy did not kneel, and when I realized Jiffy did not know what to do, and was not going to be able to do anything, I said, "I'm going to tell Mr. Patterson."

"Don't, Bobby. He'll kill Uncle Sam and they'll put Mr. Patterson in jail and he'll have a heart attack."

"You have to tell Mylinh then."

"She won't understand. In Nam, they shoot dogs and make them into hot dogs."

She crouched beside Nellie. "No one comes down here but rabbit hunters. We'll take off the dog tag in case someone finds her. Whoever finds her will think she's a stray, shot by the rabbit hunters."

As we turned away from the river and started across the field, I figured what Jiffy would do next. She would get her diary from its hiding place in the well and go into the barn and sit on the milk stool and write down the date and then write, Dear Diary, and tell the diary what had happened and then ask me to sign as a witness. She'll say, That way it's like I'm telling secrets to someone who won't tell back. You can tell me, Bobby, but I can't tell anyone, only my diary.

I knew what she would do next. She'd get the AK-47. She'd sit with it across her knee on her milking stool and wait for Uncle Sam to come back from wherever he went. She'd step through the stable door and hold the gun up to her shoulder and shoot him. And then Jiffy and me would stand together looking down at Uncle Sam in the grass and I would say, See how little the bullet hole is, no bigger than a nail hole in a board.

I went inside and climbed the stairs, but I did not set my foot on the step the church man had fixed. It was new and painted and I was afraid I would scratch it. Jiffy had forgotten to take away the matches in my jeans pocket. I could feel them rubbing against my leg as I walked along the hall. I went into the bathroom and filled the sink. After I had finished washing my hands, I went back along the hall and down the stairs.

At the bottom step, I heard Uncle Sam come back from his church group. Jiffy stood by the kitchen table drying the dishes from breakfast, a tea towel in one hand, Uncle Sam's knife in the other. She did not look brave or scared. She looked different. I hid on the bottom stair step, the door open only a crack, like Danny the Turtle peeking out of my shell, witnessing.

"I've got something for you." Uncle Sam opened the lid of a little box and held a small locket on a thin gold chain. Jiffy picked the swinging locket out of the air and studied the inscription. "This belongs to yer mother," he said. "See? Ruth McDermot. 1970. I want you to wear it to church."

He tried to open the fastener but his fingers were too big. Jiffy set the knife on the kitchen counter and took the gold chain and opened it. As she reached to put it around her neck he went around behind and held her hair aside while she fastened the clasp.

"Time for a hairdo, get the pigtails put back in it," he said.

Jiffy picked up Uncle Sam's army knife. She began drying it, back and forth along the blade, using the towel like a sharpening stone. If Mr. Patterson was there, she'd give him the knife and he'd take it from Jiffy's hand. He'd raise it over his shoulder, reach up to the ceiling, into the sky, and slice the blade down so sharp he'd slice Uncle Sam in two like a split chicken. She could write that in her diary with me signing the witness part.

She held the knife in one hand and stared at the floor with the same faraway look she gave her mother lying in her bed. The same look she gave Nellie lying in the grass. Maybe she was waiting for Uncle Sam to sit at the table and light a Cignals and then, as he sucked in a lung full of smoke, stab him in the back so that all that smoke and air would hiss out in a whistle of wrinkled rubber as Uncle Sam collapsed like an inner tube with a nail in it.

Jiffy put the knife in the drawer. She could look after me and could save baby robins, but she could not raise up from the grass a dead Nellie, and she could not lay down on the floor a dead Uncle Sam. She hung the tea towel on the rack. If she could not stab Uncle Sam with his knife, she could not shoot Uncle Sam with his gun.

THIRTY

Bobby

Uncle Sam thumped across the porch and down the steps, not noticing me, almost stepping on me. He stood in the lane reading a letter. He stuck it into his shirt pocket, at the same time bringing out his Cignals. He got into his van and started the engine. He drove out the lane onto Pork Chop Road. Behind the trees along the river, he disappeared, leaving a cloud of dust hanging above the iron bridge like smoke until long after he was gone.

I followed Jiffy's path across the field. I saw the shingled roof of the Pattersons' house. Next, I saw the steel-grey roof of the barn. The eighteen-wheeler wasn't there, which meant Mr. Patterson left early, maybe gone to Michigan to pick up some cheap bacon hogs, grunting and squealing all the way back to the packing plant the same as the regular hogs.

"He won't be back till late this afternoon," said Mrs. Patterson. "Come in, Bobby. I've just made cookies."

I sat at the table.

"My goodness, Bobby. Here it is early November and it feels like summer again. Can you believe we had snow just a week ago? One day it's one way, the next day another. You can't predict one day to the next."

"Mrs. Patterson?"

"Yes, Bobby."

"Uncle Sam shot a dog with his AK-47."

"AK-47 baloney. The gun he's got is the same as all the farmers around here have." Mrs. Patterson unlocked the cupboard next to the refrigerator. "Is it like this?" she asked, showing me Mr. Patterson's rifle.

I nodded.

"This is a single-shot Cooey .22, a farm gun. An AK-47 is an assault rifle."

"Uncle Sam shot a dog with his farm gun."

I watched her face, waiting for her to guess so I wouldn't have to tell her. She sat opposite me with her tea. "He didn't need to shoot it. He should have called me. It probably belonged to somebody. It would have had a dog tag to tell whose it was. But then again, some people, they don't want a dog and they'll drive into the country and drop it on the side of the road." She stirred her tea. Her face wasn't scowling and getting upset.

"It was Nellie."

Mrs. Patterson turned to look at the wall. She got up and looked out the window. She put the milk back in the refrigerator. She leaned her back against the counter and stood there the way she did when she was having a good look at things.

The folds under her chin were wobbling when Mrs. Patterson said, "You'd better go home now, Bobby. I'll see if I can get a hold of Mr. Patterson."

I went home and sat under the apple tree. Then I hauled hogs back and forth across the step. That one back wheel was still broken, but if I prodded the boss hog over into one corner and poked the other hogs in beside it at the back of the trailer, the truck didn't tip over.

I wandered down the lane. Because the sun was behind me, I walked on the heels of my shadow, my legs stepping when it stepped, my foot falling when it fell, as if I was following the footsteps of some other Bobby along the lane towards the barn. I left my truck on the cement ledge by the door and walked past the empty stalls and along the wall and out the back stable door. I reached into my wooden box and pulled out the newspaper and the matches and the dry sticks.

I walked through the grass to the hole in the fence and crawled through the weeds to the other side. At the hen house, I stopped. Hens were scratching in the dirt outside the pen, looking for grains of wheat to plant like in the little red hen story Jiffy was using to teach Mylinh to read. The chickens reminded her of home, she said. Most were inside the pen because it was getting dark. I peeked through the dusty window. The new rooster was in a separate pen in one corner. Seeing my shadow on the glass, he stretched his neck to watch me first with one eye, then the other. Uncle Sam called him Big Red. He said he bought him for the cockfights on the reserve, Paid big money, by Jeezus.

I dropped away from the window. In the dead hollyhocks lined up against the back wall, I crumpled the paper, piled on the sticks, and lit the match. The minute the fire jumped from the corner of the page, I felt warmth on my cheeks and hands. I crouched close to the heat. I watched the wind bend the hollyhocks against the grey boards. I sat in the circle of red light and shut my eyelids tight and listened to the flames snap like flags in the wind.

At Daddy's funeral, a black flag hung from our car aerial. As we drove down the side road to the cemetery, the flag snapped like dry kindling as long threads frayed in the wind. By the time we reached the grave, the flag was gone, blown away.

The fire grew hotter. Without opening my eyes, I shifted farther from the waving black and red flames. From inside the chicken house, I heard the hens flapping to roost, squabbling for room on the broom handle perches along the back wall. Gradually, the black and red became circles of yellow, like two suns.

A blast of heat sent me scrambling. High-pitched squawks screamed above the rattle of wings against the window. I raced to the barn for the hose. But the shrieks from the chicken house frightened me so bad that, inside the stable, I hid in an empty stall. Finally, the squawking died down. From the doorway, I saw the flames still burning along the roof and saw red balls of hen house sailing across the field. After a while, the fire stopped snapping and the smoke thinned into threads, and by the time Jiffy found me hiding in the hayloft, Uncle Sam's chicken house had blown away.

***

A knock sounded on the side door. I slipped out of bed and crept over and looked out my bedroom window at the black police car sitting in the lane.

I heard Uncle Sam call from the porch. "How you doin', Percy?"

Percy, who was fatter than Father Kelly, heaved himself out from under the steering wheel. I heard his boots clump across the porch and into the kitchen.

"Bobby, come down here."

I came down and stood in the corner.

As he plugged in the coffee maker, Uncle Sam said, "Bobby is a firebug. I was hoping you could have a little talk with him."

Percy removed his policeman's hat and sat at the kitchen table. "Warm weather we're having for November."

"Tell Bobby about firebugs."

"People who set fires go to jail, Bobby," said Percy.

"What's that called when you start a fire?" Uncle Sam unlaced his boot and put the bad foot up on a chair. The coffee pot began to gurgle.

"Arson."

"Grand arsonry."

"That's right."

"You go to jail for grand arsonry."

"Sure do."

"A children's jail," said Uncle Sam. "With little cells the size of closets and a little toilet with no lid and a little bed on the cement floor. First, they take yer mug shot and then they take yer fingerprints and then they lock you up in a cell with no windows so you can't get out and set no more fires."

"That's right," nodded Percy. "All you get to eat is bread and water."

"Sometimes you get hung for setting fires. They put a rope around yer neck like this..." Uncle Sam reached up and fastened a pretend rope. "They stand you on a chair and kick the chair away and..." Uncle Sam's head jerked to one side and his marble eye bugged out and his lungs gurgled louder than the coffee pot. "They put you in a coffin. They got children's coffins at the jail, made up and ready and waiting for the next kid who starts fires."

"I only caught one firebug in my time," said Percy.

"And he's in jail waiting in his cell to be hung." Uncle Sam sat back to light a Cignals.

Percy shifted in his chair and glanced at me sitting on the floor in the corner, knees pulled up, arms folded over my head, hiding myself like Danny the Turtle. Then he turned back to Uncle Sam. "Been playing much cards lately?"

"'Bout the same. We got a little game goin' at Beasley's. You know, nickel 'n dime stuff."

"Father Kelly phoned the other day, still bothering himself about that scratch to his car. But I think I know who did it."

"I say, lock him up in one of them cells for a few years. Serve him right."

"Where's Jiffy?" asked Percy.

"Upstairs lying down. She gets stomach aches. I'm thinking I should get her to a doctor."

"Where's Mylinh?"

"In Toronto helping at her brother's store. But usually, she's here. Jiffy and her. The two of 'em are like sisters. Jiffy taught her to read and write English. Mylinh can't read and write in her own language, but she can in English, thanks to Jiffy."

"What about Ruth? What's up with her?"

"She's coming back in a week or so. Mylinh can look after her. These Vietnamese girls, by Jeezus, they're used to hard work and looking after family, aunts, uncles, sisters. They don't send an old, sick mother to any nursing home. Everyone looks after everyone else."

"And where's Jeannie?"

"Here. Back 'n forth, comes every other day."

Percy cleared his throat. "Emma Patterson says you shot Earl's dog, Nellie."

Uncle Sam's hand that was bringing his Cignals up for a drag stopped partway. The coffee pot stopped gurgling. Everything seemed to be stopped. "I shot a stray dog trying to get into my chickens. If that was Patterson's dog, he shoulda kept it at home."

"If I was you, I'd give Earl a call. Tell him you thought Nellie was a stray. Tell him you'll get him another dog. Tell him anything. Earl is a decent man. This is farm country. We're all neighbours. We don't shoot the other guy's dog, especially if it's Earl Patterson's dog."

Uncle Sam butted his Cignals. "You're bringing up a good point. Earl Patterson's got a temper. I bet it was him, not Bobby, that burned down my chicken house. Why don't you go over and ask him?"

They had forgot about the coffee. Percy got up and put on his policeman's hat and left. I didn't have to peek out of my shell to know he'd be disappearing down Pork Chop Road in his police car on his way back to Pattersons'. I waited at the kitchen window, like Danny the Turtle, saying nothing, watching for Mr. Patterson to come across the field, a shovel over his shoulder, the twitch grass slapping at the wide bottoms of his overalls he always wore on a truck run.

And then I saw him. Probably Mrs. Patterson left a message at the hog plant, probably she left a message at the auctions in Espanola, probably she left messages all over the place, and probably he was thinking about Nellie as he lined up to cross the swing bridge in Little Current. I saw that he'd not even bothered to go into the house to change before he came for Uncle Sam.

Mr. Patterson did not knock like usual. He walked right in and laid the shovel on the kitchen table in front of Uncle Sam, still sitting in his chair drinking his hawberry and smoking his Cignals.

Mr. Patterson said, "You've got a job to finish."

Uncle Sam brushed the chunks of dried mud and hard clods off the tabletop. "Job? What job?" He tilted back his head and looked down his nose at Mr. Patterson.

"You shoot a dog, you got to bury it."

"I shot at a stray dog and scared it away. It was after my chickens. Take a walk down the river. Maybe it's still there." He flipped open the lighter and lit another Cignals. "Bobby said he thought he saw a dead dog down by the river. Maybe it's not dead. Go down and look." Uncle Sam's lips curled into a sneer as he dragged in the smoke. "Take yer shovel with you." He picked it off the table and handed it to Mr. Patterson.

"You don't like my shovel use your own. Either way, you're going to bury that dog."

"Maybe this was some other dog. There's lots of dogs around that look like Nellie. The dog I shot wasn't Nellie. Probably some hunter thought she was a groundhog."

"I checked on the way over. Her tag is missing," said Mr. Patterson. "What did you do with the tag?"

"Whoever shot the dog took the tag, like in the second war. Check with that Heinz character over at Robinson's next door to you. He was in the second war. Maybe he's got the tag."

"The Robinsons moved. Heinz is in jail."

"You get the tag and then you know for sure it was Nellie and you know for sure who shot her, the guy with the tag. Heinz more than likely."

"Heinz is in jail, where you should be."

Uncle Sam dragged on his Cignals. He did not look at Mr. Patterson. He was staring at the shovel point down on the table. "In the second war," he said, "soldiers carried shovels to bury their buddies. First, they'd take off the dog tag and then they'd dig the grave with their little shovel. In Nam we didn't carry shovels and didn't dig graves. I'd liked to have had one of those little shovels. Maybe if I had one of those little shovels, Patterson, I could bury that dog. Before Nam I'd have seen a little shovel like that and I'd have said, What's that? A girl's shovel? But now, I don' know."

Uncle Sam wiped the back of his hand across his marble eye. He butted his Cignals and stood. "Tell you what, Patterson. Bring me one of those girl's shovels and I'll bury that dog for you. In the meantime, you take this big shovel with you, and I won't lay charges for you burning down my chicken house."

Mr. Patterson did not take the big shovel. He stared at Jiffy who'd come downstairs and stood in the doorway.

Uncle Sam said, "So here's what you say in case anyone wants to know. Sam was at Beasley's playing cards and a hunter came and shot a dog and dragged it down to the river — which is where you can take yourself now with your shovel, so I don't charge you with arson. Whaddya think, Patterson, Percy's gonna dust for prints to find out who set the fire and who shot the stray dog? In Nam, they used dogs to carry bombs. They'd wrap one up in plastic with fertilizer and solvent. That's how it got started. The Peace Corps or the church or whoever sent fertilizer to the peasants living in the little villages and they used it for making bombs. So they'd wrap the dogs up and give some kid a stick of Juicy Fruit to take the dogs home to explode the minute it walked in the door."

Jiffy stood by the stove, the two men by the table. Beside Uncle Sam, Jiffy looked little. Beside Mr. Patterson, Uncle Sam looked little. I peeked out from my shell, waiting for Mr. Patterson to cave Uncle Sam's head in with his shovel. Jiffy must have been thinking she was glad she wouldn't need to load Uncle Sam into the wheelbarrow to take him to the well. Mr. Patterson would do that himself. He'd drag him by one leg to the well and drop him down, listen for the splash and then come back to the kitchen so Jiffy could make him a cup of tea.

Uncle Sam said, "Percy came over and asked me, 'Did Patterson set that fire?' So I said to Percy, 'Neighbours don't set the other guy's chicken house on fire, especially if that neighbour is Patterson.'"

"This time tomorrow." Mr. Patterson picked up the shovel and poked the pointed end into Uncle Sam's chest so hard that Uncle Sam collapsed backward into the chair.

"If that dog's not buried by tomorrow, I'll be back."

THIRTY-ONE

Rebecca

Shortly after six the next morning from the kitchen window I watched Mr. Patterson pull up the drive and park behind Uncle Sam's pickup, blocking him in. He opened the back door and, shovel laid across his shoulder, walked in. Uncle Sam was fast asleep on the living room chesterfield, wedged between the heavy armrests at either end, head tilted to one side, baseball hat half covering his face.

Mr. Patterson lifted the shovel off his shoulder and poked Uncle Sam in the leg. "I'm here about Nellie. Remember me? I want that dog buried."

I watched from the kitchen door as Uncle Sam blinked himself into focus. He looked stunned, his marble eye blank as a turned off television, the other eye shifting from Mr. Patterson to the shovel.

"Earl Patterson. Yes. That's you. Did you bring me one of those girly shovels?"

Uncle Sam stretched and yawned. "Guess not. Just a minute, then. I'll get a pad and a pen and you can give me the address of where you want me to dig." He pretended to try to get up but his body seemed to have sunk so far into the upholstery he could not move. "I need a hand up." He extended his arm.

"I'm not that stupid. Get up yourself."

He heaved himself forward. He sat on the edge of the chesterfield to tie his boot. He took one end of the leather lace in his left hand and measured the length against the lace in the right hand and loosened and pulled and measured and loosened and pulled until the one end was the same as the other end and then he did the same with the loops until they matched.

He got up. His untucked plaid shirt swung as he limped out the door and into the yard and along the lane, Mr. Patterson following. As I watched them cross the field, I could see that Mr. Patterson was having trouble keeping up, and I could see that the swing of his walk was unsteady. I ran to the kitchen cupboard and grabbed Grandma's nitro and ran to catch up. I followed them along the edge of the ravine and down the bank to walk the rocks of the riverbed into the darkness at the mouth of the bridge. I followed Uncle Sam's step, thump, step, thump, echoing dully back to me from the low ceiling of the bridge until, all the way through, I stopped.

Mr. Patterson was leaning on the shovel, clutching his chest, trying to get his breath. His face was red, and his forehead covered with sweat. Into his mouth gaping open, gasping for air, I pressed one squirt, and when he heaved for more air, one squirt on his tongue. He hung on to his shovel for support and then onto my arm as I helped him to a grassy spot on the shoreline and steadied him as he lowered himself to the ground. Then he lay down with his head on my folded coat. When from down the road came the rumble of a hog truck, Mr. Patterson closed his eyes against its whirling dust.

Not until long after the truck had rattled past, the hogs squealing, the bridge trembling, did he open his eyes and try to sit up straight. But immediately he sank down in the grass and rested his head in my lap until he'd finally caught his breath. He said, "The doctor gave me one of those. To carry with me at all times."

"And where is it?"

"At home on my dresser."

We watched another truck come by, and listened to the steady pound of the wheels as it rumbled over the beams. We listened to the clatter of trailer fading away. We watched Uncle Sam's step thump coming back, rock to rock, one weak, one strong, the heel of every other boot striking sparks from every other stone.

He stopped and knelt beside Mr. Patterson. He undid the boot. When he had finished retying the laces, he placed one hand on my shoulder to lever himself up. He adjusted his shirt and tucked the tails into his pants. He reached into his pocket for his cigarettes and took one out and tapped it three times on the face of the package. The match flared and the lighted end glowed red as it swung down from his mouth. He said, "What's the matter, Patterson? Can't keep up?"

By the time I got Mr. Patterson home he was fine. "A bit of a spell," he told Mrs. Patterson.

"Coronary heart disease is not a bit of a spell. Where was your nitro?"

THIRTY-TWO

Bobby

After supper, I went to my room and climbed into bed with all my clothes on. The electric heaters were turned up high but I was cold. My bedroom door swung open and Jiffy came in. She had a faraway look as she sat on the edge of the bed and took my hand. "If you hear a bang, it's his gun. I'm going to do it. We'll dump him down the well. We'll say we don't know where he went. We'll say he set off walking down the road. We think a hunter shot him by accident."

Jiffy's footsteps went along the hall to her bedroom. Her dresser drawer rattled open. A hanger scraped along the iron pipe in her closet. I heard Uncle Sam's Mr. Safety boots clump up the stairs, step, thump, step, thump, along the hall. He went into her room.

Right away I heard Jiffy go along the hall to the bathroom. She turned on the water. I cracked my door and listened to the swishing in the sink. She turned off the water.

I pulled the covers over my head and closed my eyes. Everything was quiet. I could still smell the smoke from the chicken house, somehow stuck in my nose, although the fire was out a long time ago.

After a while, Jiffy came out of the bathroom. I slipped out of bed and opened my door and stood there, my hand on the glass doorknob.

But she walked past me, her face white as the bathroom sink. She didn't seem to be seeing, not me, not the hallway, not anything. She made no sound as she walked barefoot to the end of the hall and disappeared down the stairs. She's going to the barn for the AK-47, I thought, as I went to the window. But I heard no door open or shut downstairs and I did not see her walk down the lane to the barn. I was cold, so without taking off my clothes, I climbed into bed again and waited.

After a while, Jiffy came back up the stairs and into my room. She pulled back the covers and climbed in beside me. I had heard no gunshot, so I knew she hadn't shot Uncle Sam. She put her arms around me and hugged me.

"I can't do it. Uncle Sam says Viet and Willie Billy and Uncle Ivan are coming." She sat up. "I've got a candle. Let's light a candle and make a wish. Candles are magical. You make a wish and blow out the candles. Or like unity candles. You carve the name of someone you love and will miss very much and will worry about what will happen to him but you can't be with him or talk to him or reach him so you carve that person's name into the candle."

She used one fingernail to carve B O B B Y into the candle. She said, "Now I light the candle and I hold the flame in my cupped hands, like this, and you close your eyes and feel the energy from my flame going into your hands and up along your arms and into your shoulders and into your heart and I say, 'These hands will find you,' and then I say, 'This heart will reach you,' and then I say, 'This flame will touch you,' and then at the end I say 'This love will be yours forever.' You say that quietly to yourself, with or without a candle, and you will feel the energy of the flame drawing the love from my heart and across my shoulders and down my arms and into your hands and into your heart."

Jiffy took my hands in both of hers. "Even though I'm gone my love will find you and you will know that I am with you and will be with you forever."

I heard voices downstairs as Willie Billy, Viet, and Uncle Ivan arrived. Holding the candle in one hand, Jiffy went to the door to listen. "They're bringing in a new freezer for all the meat they're stealing from the hog plant."

She came back to sit beside me on the bed.

"Recite the poem to me, Bobby. Jiffy had a little lamb. We'll say it together and then we'll practice the candle and then you go to sleep. Whatever happens, remember the poem. Say it. Jiffy had a little lamb. Say it with me."

∗∗∗

I woke up a little while later to a loud bang. I threw back the covers and crept down the stairs. Viet was shouting. Ivan was yelling. And Jiffy was lying face down on the floor, the rifle beside her. Willie Billy was propped against the wall, holding his foot. With the same towel Jiffy used to wipe Uncle Sam's knife, Uncle Sam tried to stop the bleeding from Willie Billy's big toe.

Uncle Sam explained to Viet. "She was in the barn and Willie Billy surprised her and she shot him in the toe. She didn't mean it."

Ivan bent over to examine what was left of Willie Billy's big toe.

"Now you got a sore toe like Viet," said Ivan.

"Say you're sorry, Jiffy," Uncle Sam pointed at Willie Billy's toe. "Tell him you're sorry."

But Jiffy, now curled up crying in one corner, said nothing.

"We better take him to the hospital," said Ivan.

"He's illegal." Uncle Sam folded the towel to a dry spot. "Don't matter. He'll be all right. Hold the towel for me. I got painkillers for my foot."

Willie Billy chased down the painkillers with a glass of hawberry. Uncle Sam picked up the AK-47 and left, probably returning it to its hiding spot in the barn. Jiffy brushed past me and went upstairs. When Uncle Sam returned, the men went back to what they were doing.

Uncle Ivan said, "We got all this meat. We got two freezers to put it in. But I had a look downstairs. All the circuits have fifteen-amp fuses. Every time a freezer and a baseboard heater kick on together a fuse will blow. You need twenty-amp fuses."

"Viet knows about wiring," said Uncle Sam. "That was his job in Nam, wiring booby traps. He'd use WD–1 commo wire and two hours later a fire'd start. He planted booby traps in the dead bodies of American soldiers, and when Charlie tried to steal their watches, they'd blow up, how the time flies. So he's going to bypass the fuse and wire the freezers direct into sixty-amp service."

Uncle Sam patted the shiny white top. "Twenty-four cubic foot. That's gonna hold a lot of pork chops."

I went back to bed. I could hear them laughing and talking, doing their wiring and drinking their hawberry and smoking their Cignals and laughing some more about Willie Billy's toe. "It's a good thing it wasn't his willy," Uncle Sam said about twenty times. Then Ivan and Viet and Willie Billy left. I crept along the hall to Jiffy's room, but she told me to go away. I stood in the dark behind the door of my bedroom, waiting until Jiffy's door opened and her footsteps padded along the hall to the bathroom. When the door closed behind her, I slipped into her room. But when I heard Uncle Sam's Mr. Safeties clumping up the stairs, I ran back to my bedroom. Uncle Sam came along the hallway. Through the crack in my door, I watched him sit on Jiffy's bed and drink from his bottle, almost emptying it.

I crept along the hall but the bathroom was empty, so I went down the stairs to the kitchen. Jiffy was not there either. As I was about to start up the stairs, I heard Uncle Sam's footsteps on the floor above. I crouched on the bottom step. When the footsteps came along farther and started down the stairs, I ran outside and stood in the long grass near the back. Maybe Jiffy had gone to the stable for the AK-47.

As I headed for the barn I began to shiver, the cold creeping down my neck and along my back and down to my legs to my shoes, which were wet from the dew.

I thought I could smell smoke.

Under the full moon, I could see the apple tree standing in the shadows of the house, which stood before the big trees along Pork

Chop Road. The living room lights, shining through the curtains covering the side windows, blinked off. The light above the back door blinked off, as though Uncle Sam, sitting in the kitchen, had got tired waiting up for me and gone to bed.

I crept across the yard to sit under the apple tree. From a change in the moon, the night seemed suddenly bright as day. As I crept along the lane, I felt someone watching, maybe Jiffy. She's up there, in the bedroom window. Maybe Daddy, up there in Heaven watching me climb the steps and creep across the porch. I tiptoed up the stairs to listen. From the rooms along the hallway came no sound. I snuck down the steps. I thought I could smell something burning, not wood or cigarettes or matches but something like a crackling splutter of smoking sparks trying to turn into fire. I returned to the stable to wait.

The stable door opened. Jiffy saw me but did not stop. She went to the grain bin, but the gun wasn't there. She searched around, finding it finally next to a hay bale. She slipped open the bolt. As she walked past me, I saw that her expression was not brave and not frightened, but far away, like when she had the army knife. She wore the same jeans with the big pockets and the same blue T-shirt and blue winter coat she wore when we'd found Nellie. She shut the stable door behind her.

I smelled a different smoke. I went to the stable door. There was no light in the kitchen window. The upstairs windows in a dark row stared down on me. I sniffed at the wind as it changed direction, filling my nose with the hog plant, or maybe with the smell of hay bales gone mouldy in a field somewhere, left there for a winter home for the field mice. I felt like they were watching me, peeking out a hay bale window, wondering why I was standing all alone in the yard, instead of being in my house for the winter.

Then I saw in my bedroom window what looked like my dad's hand come down from Heaven to strike a match and touch a flame to Jiffy's candle and hold it to the edge of my blue curtains, where the wick fluttered like a moth at a light. Next, in Jiffy's window, the same candle in the same hand touched the flame to her pink curtains. Then in the living room, by the same candle in the same hand, the curtains leaped into flames.

The fires blinked out. My dad had seen Jiffy was there in her room and put the fires out. I could still smell the smoke so I knew the fires must be in there somewhere, in the walls and in the closets, looking for bedbugs. That was why my dad had come down from Heaven, to kill the bedbugs so they wouldn't get into Jiffy's bed.

I decided to go back to the house. I had almost reached the apple tree when I saw showers of sparks on the kitchen curtains leap into flames. All the windows lit up as fire burst from one corner of the roof and ran with the wind along the eaves in a race along the ridge, hissing under the shingles so loud I had to hold my hands over my ears as the heat smashed out the glass of every window. Tongues of red reached left and right and turned the back half of the house to orange as the roof snapped in two and collapsed into a wall of sparks reaching from the top of the chimney to the bottom of the basement. I watched as the walls melted and crumbled and the house tumbled to pieces. Only the chimney stood like a square black post in the flames.

I hid there like Danny the Turtle under the apple tree, peeking out, watching the black smoke drift from red coals. Then the wind sprang up and a cloud of sparks leaped from the smoke and the fire boiled up again. I ran, not knowing in the dark where to go until I reached the iron bridge. I slid down the river bank and hid where I built my fires. A police car, its sirens wailing and lights flashing hubdubbed overhead, knocking dirt and gravel onto my face and hair. I climbed the bank and stared across the field at the smoking chimney. I heard more sirens screaming from beyond the hog plant and down Pork Chop Road. I ran under the bridge to hide behind a log that lay near the water. More sirens came from another direction, ringing across the planks above my head.

I climbed the bank. But no sooner had I reached the roadside than I heard two more. I ducked behind the log and again, through the iron beams, the sirens sounded, peeling together overhead and screaming towards the house, showering me in dirt. After a while, thinking it was safe, I climbed up the bank for the third time. I watched the sparks blown by the wind float from the house, lighting the yard filled with fire trucks and police cars. Too late, I heard footsteps slapping through the grass.

"Bobby, here you are. Omigod, Bobby. I've been looking for you." Jiffy crouched beside me and hugged me. "Don't cry, Bobby. This is good. He'll think we got trapped in the fire. He'll think we're dead."

"I'm cold."

She wrapped her arms around me tighter. "If he thinks we're dead, that's good, because now we're safe, we're dead witnesses. Up in smoke, like the bedbugs, Bobby. You did it. Up in smoke, Bobby. No more bedbugs."

"Where is Uncle Sam?"

"He's looking for us. They're all looking for us."

Jiffy took off her jacket and fastened it around my shoulders. She hugged me. She rocked me. She didn't look like Jiffy anymore. She sounded older. "The Espanola auctions are tomorrow. We'll hide in Mr. Patterson's hog trailer. From Espanola we'll disappear, somewhere they can't find us, disappeared like Mrs. Patterson's lost children."

"I didn't start the fire. It was my dad. He killed the bedbugs."

We started walking in the other direction, Jiffy explaining: "I thought about Mylinh when I saw Nellie lying in the grass. I thought about her lying in the ditch in Nam. I thought the next one will be Bobby lying in the ditch, and I remembered Uncle Sam's story about his buddy hanging off a fence and how Uncle Sam pulled off his dog tag. I remembered he gave me this necklace, which was like a dog tag, and I thought next thing it'll be me hanging off the fence. I remembered I got Nellie's dog tag in my pocket, and I thought it's like I got Uncle Sam's dog tag in my pocket. I decided to leave the necklace and the dog tag in the hayloft where Nellie had her pups where Mr. Patterson will eventually find it. Like some other say. He will understand this means we're not dead and without telling anyone will come looking for us."

I could smell the smoke in the air and, looking back, I could see it rising and disappearing through that doorway in the clouds. At last, I saw the roof of the Pattersons' barn. Jiffy took my hand and we went through the field and around the back of the barn. She hoisted me high enough to open the latch of the trailer and we climbed inside.

"When Mr. Patterson comes, you can't say anything. Not now. He'll go looking for Uncle Sam. He'll kill himself looking for Uncle Sam, or else Uncle Sam will kill him first."

Jiffy put her arms around me and hugged me and rocked me. She wasn't crying and her voice wasn't shaking, and she seemed like a big sister only all of sudden bigger.

"That girl Carly, Verna's daughter, said she'll help us. Mylinh will help us. Aunt Jeannie lives in Regent Park. Mrs. Patterson said Sarah lives in Regent Park too. Someone will help us."

"My dad started the fire to kill the bedbugs."

"We'll hide here in the trailer and drive with Mr. Patterson to the auction. We'll follow that road into town to the Greyhound bus depot. I've got your money from the Jiffy jar. We'll buy a ticket to Toronto and we'll go to Regent Park."

"My dad started the fire so you wouldn't get bedbugs in your bed."

She let go of me. She looked away, almost saying something, I don't know what. When she looked back at me, she reminded me of sitting in our favourite spot next to a loose floorboard in the hayloft of the Pattersons' barn, passing those big candies back and forth until they were sucked to nothing. I thought that was where she'd hidden the crowbar, under that loose floorboard. She would sometimes poke her finger in and pick up one end of the board to peek inside. What are you looking for? I'd ask. Nothing, she'd say. But her eyes would grow kind of far away like they did when she was planning something so then I knew she told me that in case I told Uncle Sam.

She said, "I think I might have started the fire. The candles, Bobby. I forgot to blow them out. Or maybe the bad wiring started the fire. I don't know. All I know is you didn't start the fire."

THIRTY-THREE

Bobby

The tires crunched to a stop. Boots slap slapped in the twitch grass. Through the slats of the trailer, I saw Mr. Patterson and two other men checking out the pigs in outdoor pens, waiting to be loaded. For protection against dirt swirling up from the road, we'd travelled with our sweaters over our faces, like Uncle Sam covered his in the tunnels in Nam. Mr. Patterson had changed the straw in the trailer after his last run, but he hadn't hosed the trailer down because of the frost so we were filthy and smelled like pigs.

I sank into the bed of straw, hugging myself for warmth. I thought about Nellie. I pictured her still lying stretched out flat in the grass, looking like she was sleeping, except for the bullet hole Uncle Sam put in her head. It was hardly bleeding, no bigger than a nail hole in a board. I thought about the farmhouse, burned to the ground now. I thought of the curtains Mylinh had made, gone up in smoke now. I thought about being an arsonist, locked in a jail.

"Danny Turtle, you're shaking! My goodness, you're freezing!" Jiffy began to rub my back and shoulders through my jacket, like rubbing Danny's shell. Stretching my neck and peeking out, I could see the blue buttons of her blue coat floating like tiny boats on a pond, one after the other rising and falling with the movement of her arm.

"We'll have to get you a good wool sweater and another blanket. This one's too thin. Give me your hands. Let me warm them up."

"We don't have any blankets."

"It's a pretend blanket."

She took my hands. She sat back for a closer look at me. "My goodness, what long eyelashes. They make you look dreamy. But you're not feeling too dreamy, I bet."

She hugged me and rocked me. After a while, my legs aching from what seemed like two hours of crouching in the straw, I got up and came out of my shell and peeked through the slats. The auction was a big square house with a chimney up one side. Through the front window I could see people walking around. If I looked up, a light above the door shone into my eyes. The door was so small, Mr. Patterson would have to bend over to fit through it. And his hog truck wouldn't fit anywhere except where it was.

I wanted to call to Mr. Patterson and explain. At first, Mr. Patterson wouldn't say anything. He'd look down at me. But then he would take my hand and say, "The fire was not your fault, Bobby."

Uncle Sam would not reach down and take my hand. He would phone Percy, the policemen.

"How did the fire start?" Percy would ask.

"My dad was killing the bedbugs."

"Why were you hiding in this trailer?"

"Me and Jiffy are running away."

"If you didn't light the fire, why are you running away? And that scratch on Father Kelly's car? What about that, Bobby?"

Percy would take me to the jail where he would ask the same questions again and write the answers down in his report and make me sign it and then take my fingerprints and put me in the little cell built for children waiting to be hung.

Jiffy poked me. Mr. Patterson was there, looking down, as though he'd asked me something. He said, "They figure your Uncle Sam is buried in the rubble but they can't dig him out until it cools down."

He gave me a hand up. "So, Big Guy, if you're strong enough and brave enough to come this far, you're strong enough to take an eight-mile bus ride home. Emma is waiting."

He motioned for us to follow. We crawled to the back of the trailer, lowered ourselves over the edge and dropped to the ground. Jiffy took my hand. As we walked across a parking lot, she brushed the dirt and the straw off us both. But she could not brush off the smell of pig, now mixed and soaked into our clothes along with the smoke. We followed Mr. Patterson into the auction office to keep warm while they loaded the hogs.

THIRTY-FOUR

Rebecca

I had known that if we followed the gravel road from the auctions, we would come to a sign pointing the way to Espanola. I knew the bus station was at the Red and White. I was certain that in Toronto, I would find my way to Carly's house and then she would help me find Aunt Jeannie and Sarah. I didn't know how but I would have. I knew that because, compared to all the stuff I had done up to now, it seemed to me as easy as finding their names in a phone book.

But now, waiting for the bus to take us back to where we came from, me sitting beside Mr. Patterson, who was holding onto our tickets, I began to think about it more. In the trailer, Bobby had shook from the cold. The farm kid stink of pigs was so strong the bus driver might not have sold us a ticket. I wouldn't be able to keep up my Now-I-am-Rebecca front. I might not have been able to find Aunt Jeannie or Sarah. If a policeman had found us on the street, our clothes dirty from the stock truck, our hair matted with road dust, and Bobby pale, skinny and frightened — straight to Children's Aid.

Mr. Patterson led us to the front of the store so Bobby could look at the statue in front of Webbwood Post Office, next door to the Manitoulin Hardware.

But he wasn't interested.

"Let's play Danny the Turtle," I said. "Say hello when I knock." I tapped his head. "Are you home, Danny?"

No response.

"No matter how many inches you roam, Danny, you will always have a home." I tapped again. "Are you almost home, Danny?"

No answer.

"Even if you go a hundred inches you will always have a home."

No interest.

"Here is Danny." I formed a fist and stuck out a thumb. "You do the same."

Bobby formed a fist and stuck out a thumb.

"So let's go home." I folded my thumb into my fist and Bobby folded his thumb into his fist.

That's when Mr. Patterson said, "You've been hiding in your turtle house all this time, Bobby, but you don't need to hide anymore." Mr. Patterson poked out his thumb and Bobby poked out his thumb and after a while he fell asleep. When the bus arrived, we waved bye-bye to Mr. Patterson and climbed on.

The bus wandered through some small towns and then across the swing bridge at Little Current. I closed my eyes and listened to the hum of the tires. I thought about what Mr. Patterson would be doing now, his shirt sleeves rolled up, his arms and face brown from the winter wind, loading the hogs, exactly what he was not supposed to do. I pictured what Mrs. Patterson would be doing now, sitting at the kitchen table, her face pale in comparison to Mr. Patterson's, wearing her glasses, putting on the kettle, pouring the water into the white teapot, waiting for us to arrive, exactly what she was supposed to do.

Then the cold fingers of Uncle Sam catching his bedbugs pushed the Pattersons aside and a chill crept up the back of my neck and down to my belly to tighten my stomach into knots as I saw Uncle Sam coming through the grass and I heard him clumping across the laneway gravel and I saw from the fall of every other step his big boot sparking from the rocks. For me he was still alive, still that marble eye staring at me: By Jeezus, yer a cutie.

I opened my eyes.

The fat woman who had got on the bus in Little Current sat beside me and Bobby, making the seat seem too narrow. The big hardcover book in the woman's lap seemed to be squeezing my legs against the bus wall. The arm, which poked into my space each time the woman moved strands of hair away from her face to tuck under a bobby pin, seemed to shrink the bus smaller.

Like a shoelace, a bobby pin has two ends turned back upon each other, one side straight as a fence line and the other lined with little humps, like furrows in a field fresh plowed after all the rocks thrown up by the frost like frozen memories have been loaded into the wagon and piled at the back of the field. The humpy part was behind me now but not the memories.

"Pork Chop Road?" the driver asked.

"It's regional road something. I'll tell you when we get there. We can walk from there."

We got off the bus and I took Bobby's hand and we started along the shoulder of the road. At Leonard's lane I hung back. I told Bobby to go on ahead to the Pattersons'. I needed to look around. I didn't know what for. I just knew I needed to do it.

THIRTY-FIVE

Bobby

While Mrs. Patterson ran the bathwater, I stood at the door waiting.

"You're shy, Bobby. I know, but you can't take a bath with your clothes on. You'd rather be by yourself. Would you rather be by yourself? Or do you want me to help?"

I shrugged. "I don't know."

"You're going to need a good scrub. And a hair wash. So don't be shy. Just pretend we're all girls here."

Mrs. Patterson shut the door. "Well then. Let's do it. Oh my, it's okay for little boys to be filthy but not this little boy. I got some bubble bath here, the foamy stuff. It looks sort of funny but it foams up. Foam up is for girls, I know, but look how it foams up, is that ever going to feel good. You just sit in there and I'll sit here on the john and then we'll wash your hair and you'll feel like a new person. I can give you a manicure to clean those fingernails. But we got our work cut out for us, that's for sure."

The water was hot and the bubble bath smelled like pine trees but I was too tired to pick up the soap.

"Let me help a little. Use a little Rinso. Let Rinso wash your cares away. That used to be the commercial."

Mrs. Patterson soaped the face cloth and began to wash, first my back, and then my arms and then down along my legs. She hooked up a spray thing to the tap and soaped and rinsed my hair. She handed me the soap. "Now you do your feet. Get between those toes. That's where the dirt hides."

As I scrubbed and cleaned, I felt tears come up, but I was too tired to cry.

"All clean now. All right. Let's dry you off."

Mrs. Patterson wrapped the towel around me and began to rub, starting with my hair and then down along my back to my waist and my legs. "This is how you're supposed to dry yourself. You start at the top and work your way down … What is that?" She pointed at the red mark on my leg.

"A mosquito bite, I think," I said.

"All right. For a minute I thought … What's this here? What's the matter with this picture? It's too cold for mosquitos. And look here. These red marks. How did you get those?"

My spots were red, but they weren't itchy.

"These are bedbug bites, Bobby."

Mrs. Patterson stared at me. She leaned close to touch the marks with her finger tips. "My God. Those are bedbug bites."

THIRTY-SIX

Rebecca

The lane of Leonard's farm looked the same as yesterday. But the house was gone, all but the foundation. The farm equipment that was there yesterday was there today. The plowed fields not growing anything were there yesterday and there today, still not growing anything. Some boards of the barn that were gone yesterday were still gone today, and some shingles of the barn roof were gone yesterday and still gone today. Everywhere I looked seemed like picking up a postcard of a place I'd been to long ago, but long ago was only yesterday. Yesterday, over there in the grass, Bobby had been sitting, watching me from under his eyelashes, and over there was the path to the barn waiting for me like yesterday. Nothing in these postcards had changed. But what I came for from yesterday was missing.

The stable door squeaked open on stiff hinges, the same as yesterday, and swung into a gloom of cold dusty cobwebs the same as yesterday. Waving my arms in front of me to brush aside the cobwebs that had been there yesterday, I saw through the little window to my right, smoky from dirt, a patch of blue sky. I wiped away the grime on the glass so I could see the swallows circling in and out through a missing board, gliding away, disappearing, circling back, not really the same as yesterday because yesterday the grime was too thick to see through. But they were there, against a patch of blue, the same as yesterday.

I followed the stone wall past the standing stalls to the chink in the foundation. I closed my eyes and reached in, afraid to touch the hardened blood-smeared metal of the crowbar, but it was there. Like yesterday.

I left the stable, Uncle Sam's crowbar dangling from my left hand. I crossed through the twitch grass to the well. I lifted out the stone and felt inside. I did not want to look at the postcard memories the diary was going to bring back from yesterday. I did not want to open those pages filled with words written by the nine-year-old fingers of a nine-year-old mind trying to understand the Uncle Sam behaviours that curled my nine-year-old me up on my bed with stomach aches that had been there for as many yesterdays as I could remember.

The sentence on the inside cover read: "Memories work backward and forwards. When these pages come together, our memories will have joined together." That had been there yesterday and was there today. I had written that for Bobby. I opened to the first page. "Dear Jiffy. You drink from your own well. The thoughts you think go down into the well and when you send down the bucket these thoughts are what come back. Think of them as wishes. You don't wish bad wishes because you don't want the bad to come back to you. You don't think bad thoughts because you don't want the bad to come back to you. May all the wishes you write in this diary be good, and may all your thoughts that fill these pages be good so that all that comes up to you from your well is good." Mrs. Patterson had written that. I opened the diary to the middle page between my thoughts and the thoughts I had written for Bobby, which I now knew were not dissolved like one thing into another but blended like two things together, for our thoughts, like our memories, like the ink that wrote them, whether back half or front half, were drawn from the same well. I had written that some long ago yesterday but I was reading it today.

I returned to the stable door, went part way in and came back out for a fresh look. I stared at the stone foundation of the house and tried to shake off the feeling that if I went over and looked, I would see coming from beneath that load of rubble a glimmer of light, which would lead me to what I was looking for. I had written about a glimmer of light in my diary, standing by the well looking down into the dark and seeing a glimmer of light waiting for me down there in my well. I could remember writing this but not like the way I could remember the AK-47 and the crowbar, not like remembering what happened to Bobby's toy truck, left somewhere, if he didn't come back for it, which I knew he wouldn't, rusting away to nothing somewhere along the lane, maybe rusting away to nothing by the river under the bridge, maybe rusting away to nothing under the rubble of the house. Not that kind of memory, not a for-sure-accurate memory but a glimmer of a more-or-less-accurate memory that what I was looking for I would find in a glint of light. Like when you close your eyes and turn away you can still see behind your eyes a glint of what you just saw.

In the sparks flying up in the gravel laneway, I had seen a hundred miles of those foot beat glints that I knew were too big to fit into any bucket, which meant they couldn't follow me down the well. So, when I was not hiding under Bobby's eyelashes, I was in the bucket going down hundreds of miles into the well. I thought that when Uncle Sam peeked over the edge he wouldn't see that far down but I would be able see that far up and what I would see was a glint, not from that marble eye and not from the sparks off his boots beats, but a glint from something else.

I went back into the stable and came out again for another look. What I was missing was here yesterday but gone today, like stones in the field that were here yesterday but gone today. There seemed to be a watch somewhere as big as the Little Current clock tower, not chiming the hour and marking the time because time had stopped because something was missing today that was here yesterday.

In the funeral parlor, as the organists played a hymn about the eternal journey, the visitors had lined up to take a peek at Leonard lying there in his coffin, like pay-your-five-cents-each one-at-a-time next-in-line. I took a peek then, not because I wanted to take a last look at him, but to make sure the envelope would survive in that airless box until, although I dreaded the thought, until the time came to reach into that box now filled with maggots with the same thumb and finger that had put in the envelope.

So I dreaded the thought of reaching into the pile of rubble now with this same thumb and finger. But when I saw in the rubble a glint of something, and when leaning down close, I saw that the glint was from the ring given to Uncle Sam by the pope and I saw that the maggots I was afraid to touch had not arrived yet and had not got started yet and I saw that what had stopped almost everything about Uncle Sam's eternal journey was that the bad foot was buried in a tangle of burned beams more twisted and snarled than the roots of that willow tree, making it impossible for anyone to pull him free, and making it totally impossible for him to ever get free.

Yet all of what he had been was gone. That was what was missing. His baby must have taken all that was him back to Nam so she could finish burning him in My Lai.

Doublewalkers. Grandma said the word came from the German doppelganger, meaning your spirit double who walked with you in your parallel universe. I thought Grandma meant your spirit double was always good. But now I knew she meant it could be the friend who walked beside you or an enemy who followed behind you or something indefinable you couldn't see and couldn't know if it was a friend or not. I think Grandma already knew that, and that was the reckoning she could see coming, and that was the smudge she was trying to rub off her coffee cup.

THIRTY-SEVEN

Rebecca

I wrote in my diary that if I had a ladder, I could lower it rung by rung to rest on the bottom with the ladder almost straight up and down, and with just the right amount of room for me, only nine years old, to lower myself partway on the upside, and then, close to the stone wall, climb around to the downside, finally reaching the water, which was probably no more than up to my knees. From there I could look up, and because I was looking up, I could see and understand who my Doublewalker was and why she was here.

I sat on the stone wall of the well, diary in one hand, crowbar in the other. This was not an ordinary well. There was no bucket perched on the edge of the stone wall with a large iron crank waiting for me to lower it. There was no rattle of the bucket and no grating of a crank that brought up from the blackness whatever besides water was down there. But once I got down there what I might see and understand was how a baby that didn't exist could put a smudge that didn't exist on Grandma's coffee cup and a smell that didn't exist in my nose.

Had Uncle Sam never arrived on my doorstep, I would never have met that baby. Mylinh told me. By Jeezus yer a cutie, Uncle Sam would say, as he rocked his little baby and sang that little girl with pigtails song.

I held the diary over the dark hole and held my breath and listened to the moments of silence before the splash. Careful not to touch the crusted blood, using the sharp end of the crowbar as a pry, I began one by one to loosen the rocks of the stone wall, toppling each down to land first with a splash and then with a dull thud until the hole was filled and all that was Uncle Sam was buried underneath so much dead weight that no memories and no smell and no bedbugs could ever seep or creep or climb back to the surface and into my mind. Not totally gone, mind you. Nothing that lives will ever be totally gone, especially not a baby.

I started off down Pork Chop Road, walking slowly until it dropped down to the plank bridge. I stopped. Under it, the river wound its way across fields and through trees and appeared again at another bridge where maybe another six-year-old boy now played with matches, and maybe another big sister now scolded him for lighting fires.

I looked into the uncracked mirror below, the water still and deep and peaceful because it was November, and the banks were full but the current not fast like in March. Above my reflection, the afternoon sky was growing heavy with clouds piling up and rolling together and grumbling themselves into rain. I remembered Bobby looking up to the sky trying to find the door his father went through into Heaven. Now, looking up, I could see no door. But now, looking down, I could see myself. And I knew if I looked long enough into myself, I would see a door, and if I opened that door and if I went through that door, I might see the baby that Uncle Sam saw in me. She's in my well somewhere.

THIRTY-EIGHT

Rebecca

I follow Bobby up the staircase with the banister polished and shining in the light of the newly painted hallway. I imagine the ordinary happy families that must have lived in this old farmhouse, the innocent little feet that must have run along this hallway and up and down these steps. The little girls in pigtails and ribbons hiding in secret places from little boys in scuffed sneakers, no worries or fears in this place of safety. One of those pigtailed little girls on sunny afternoons would be in the yard just out the back door. She would be finding that baby robin under that bush, waiting with wings already flapping in anticipation of her bending down with cupped hands to pick it up and cradle it in a little box while those sneaker-footed boys poked into the fresh-turned garden soil for worms that would curl and twist until the least sissy of the boys broke it in pieces for the waiting baby.

Now I feel safe. Not because I am at the Pattersons' with no more worries about Uncle Sam, but because every night in the rustling of the summer breeze in the curtains of my new bedroom window I can hear the soft sighs of Bobby's breathing. But like Mylinh told me would happen, sometimes I wake up at three in the morning and I see the baby at my bedside. But she doesn't bother me, and she doesn't stay. When she's satisfied there are no bedbugs left to bite me, that the fire burned them all, she drifts across the room, out the window, and down the lane, going the other way. But in the shaft of light coming from the rubble of that farm house she stops and turns to me and says, Serves him right, by Jeezus.

END